MEMORIES LAST LONGEST

Edward & Elizabeth Anderson

authorHOUSE®

AuthorHouse™ UK
1663 Liberty Drive
Bloomington, IN 47403 USA
www.authorhouse.co.uk
Phone: 0800.197.4150

Published by AuthorHouse 10/28/2016

ISBN: 978-1-5246-6465-7 (sc)
ISBN: 978-1-5246-6466-4 (hc)
ISBN: 978-1-5246-6470-1 (e)

Print information available on the last page.

Introduction

Thyself with Shining Foot Shall Pass.

Two years before the outbreak of War events pointed in that direction. In 1937 American President Roosevelt wanted the peace loving nations to quarantine the aggressive German Japan and Italy, to avoid the approaching Perils. American journalist Howard K Smith noted four observations on the new Germany. 1. The admiration for German neatness, efficiency, prosperity and cleanliness wrongly crediting these characteristics to Hitler. 2. The marching in uniforms and the open display of guns. All the Heil Hitler salutes and military pageantry which was exciting to see. 3. The strange stark terror of perceiving what was happening to Germans. 4. The fear and realisation the rest of the world did not comprehend the danger Hitler posed. Most Americans did not progress beyond stage 2.

In France the 1937 cinema film Jean Renoir's 'The Grand Illusion' examines Europe through the lens of the First World War and the contemporary rise of fascism. The story has a human side. That of simply choosing the ending of all wars or we say goodbye to our beautiful world.

Japan goes to war with China 1937 and by the end of the year capture Shanghai, Beijing and Nanking. Princess Chichibu of the Japanese Imperial family visits Britain representing Japan for the Coronation of the George VI. She has a great love for America and England.

Germany has reached a decision to sterilize all coloured children. A new order from the German Ministry of the Interior deprives all Jews of Municipal Citizenship. German warplanes carry out the first bombing in history of an undefended town. More than 1,600 people of Guernica are killed. April 1937.

Britain 1937 King Edward VIII abdicates for love. Neville Chamberlain became Prime Minister, soon after had the Factories Act passed limiting the hours worked by Women and Children. Chamberlain believed he could make Germany a stable partner in Europe, Germany would settle down with the restoration of a few colonies. Many Debutants of England paid the occasional visit to Germany for a Romance.

'Once In a While, Farewell my Love, Ebb Tide' was the three of the top music hits of 1937.

There was still a genuine hope of avoiding war and on the last day of 1938 Mr Chamberlain hoped the next year would be not only peaceful, but a happy one for everyone. He had said with some optimism, "I can assure you the Government for which I am speaking will do its upmost to make it so."

1.

Departing Days.

Cameron thought his father David Andrews was the most relaxed man he ever knew. He would take off his watch at meal times to place it on its side as if to banish the spell of time. Then he would chat humorously to all at his table where only the topic seems to exist and time elsewhere. That Sunday in September 1939 he outlined his plan to make Cameron a local reporter in his own beloved Lothian Despatch newspaper. The newspaper was his life's work and with all its difficulties and daily challenges which he had to overcome his laid-back character remained like a rock. The building was an old flower mill situated near a river and had a rustic narrow bridge next to where a Victorian family had a stable for their coach horses. The stable had a large clock on a central tower that still chimed on the hour. David looked at his son with approval and said, "You have earned a chance in my industry for the years you helped print the best rag in the midlands and borders of Scotland." Then David turned to Geordie who was in a day dream and caught in surprise, "you will also join the Dispatch and its motley crew." At that point David stood up and saluted Geordie and Cameron saying. "We are glad to have you on board our good ship 'gossip'." He said this with a wink and a warm smile. Around the table was his aristocratic wife Clarinda who leaned over to hold the hand of her husband and son Cameron. She was the older sister of a Laird and could remember the contemporary Queen as a little girl. She liked to tell the story of an amphitheatre built especially for Queen Victoria. It was close to where the boughs of the riverbank trees dipped into the slow moving waters. It was across from the old round steam heated building for the growth of oranges.

On the stone stage of the amphitheatre the young Queen played Sherlock Homes and Clarinda Professor James Moriarty. Dramatic scenes of dagger fights to the death were played to a local audience of well-heeled aristocrats, tweed clad game keepers, rough and muddy farm workers with their ponies accompanied by their barking dogs.

Making up the numbers at the Andrews table were Cameron's old childhood and school friends. Robert Mason sleek and handsome his dark hair flopping over his eyes as if it somewhere they had to hide. It seemed Robert had never changed since he and Cameron first met. Some ten years before Cameron was swinging on a rope tied to an overhanging branch. The long springy branch allowed a swinger to skim over the river and land place on a large rock. Robert came ambling along the riverside path and saw the rope swing in action and became desperate to have a try. He had on his best Sunday suit but nevertheless decided in his teen wisdom he must have a go. He threw himself with all his strength at the rope and swerved over the toffee coloured river spinning like a frantic top. Robert completely missed the large rock and swung back knee deep through the river. Robert could feel the water splash up to his braces and soak his white Sunday shirt tail. Cameron laughingly congratulated Robert on his acrobatic skills and would recommend him for a job when the circus came to town. Cameron wanting to show his skill made a wild grab sending him gracefully over the river sounding like Jonny Weissmuller (Tarzan) until the branch yielded to his weight. Cameron hit the water sideways splashing water high up the embankment. When he managed to pull himself out and climb up to Robert where he was met with a wild laughter. "When the circus comes to town well both get a job washing the elephants."

The summer sun stayed on the horizon warming the wet boys and partly drying their cloths as they lay in the grass. The clouds were white as if they had been laundered amid a soft blue sky. Cameron was the first to talk hoping not to break the summer spell. "We have a stove at the newspaper mill; it won't take long to light. What do you say old man?" Robert did not fancy the idea of facing his mother with the Sunday suit wrinkled and smelling of damp and gladly nodded in agreement. Cameron took Robert to the paper mill and set the pot-bellied stove alight. The stove was in the Despatch printing room surrounded by machinery piles of paper. Robert soon began feeling at home because he had found a trusted friend.

He was proud to introduce his sister Molina the next day, who because of her good looks and natural female charm played the devil with men; a glance often sent men into a spin. Robert even including amongst her admirers was the young confessional priest who blushed at the sight of her, making it obvious to all and sundry he still had the feelings of a man. Cameron, because of his new friend Robert wanted to accept Molina as a sister of a kind and yet he was drawn strangely to her as soon as she appeared in a room. When Molina addressed Cameron it took a lot of self-control to appear unaffected while his heart and body sometimes forgot the rules. At that point he would make some excuse to leave and then retreat promptly leaving behind a rather puzzled Molina.

Larry Goodman and Cameron were old firm friends and had shared a hobby of exchanged comic books and ideas all through their school days. Larry was an avid collector and had in perfect order piles of comics ready for exchange usually for a decent profit. Larry was the natural athlete of the bunch with dark eyebrows that met in the middle, square jaw and high cheekbones. He was a champion swimmer, 100 yard sprinter and middle distance runner of admirable stamina. They were all proud to know him as a friend and banded together enthusiastically to cheer him in athletic events, he was their personal hero.

Geordie McWilliams was the quiet man who examined the world around him with caution and concern. Cameron had met him in the local boxing club on Saturday morning. The club instructor was tidying up the apparatus with only a few minutes to go before the end of the session. He was watching them workout when he decided to make them fight each other for three rounds. He explained his intention was to find a good fight to begin this year's boxing tournament and considered they would fit the bill. Geordie and Cameron had become close chums and naturally did not want to hurt each other and danced around ducking and weaving. The instructor, as soon as he noticed this shouted, "If you don't put some life into it I'll box both your ears." Not wishing to put it to the test they threw themselves into a fully-fledged fight. Geordie was good in the attack while Cameron excelled in retaliating. Soon their determination and skills began attracting the other members of the club to watch. The dust beams shone in the sunlight from the overhead glass roof. Like a powerful searchlight the sunlight covered the fighters in a silvery glow as they battled from one corner to another. By the third round Cameron had a slight lead but as the moments passed Geordie caught up in constant attacks and so the points swayed from one to another. At the end of the three rounds fighting it was impossible to say with honesty which of them had won. The instructor just nonchalantly told them they were well matched knowing this would make the first fight of as good as you could get. He was right; the display brought the audience to their feet and loud applauds resounded in appreciation for both of them. The fight was declared a draw and bets were already on the table who would win the next fight.

2.
Correspondents on the Rise.

Geordie was a cub reporter along with Cameron; both had stained their fingers in printing ink working on the paper since high school. The digging out a story that would interest the public and sell papers plus the excitement of a deadline made for profitable days, much more than ordinary work. They were both very proud of being real reporters after the years of study and working in the old mill with its industrial air and the clutter of the machines churning out their work seven days a week.

They had worked long hours at the works and had plodded the over the countryside in sun, snow and rain looking for any story, always hoping for a break. Their first contact had been the famous local Sergeant Brown of the Border Police Force who advised them to buy a sturdy bicycle like a Rudge-Whitworth; he explained it was a bonus to be able to cycle on a machine you can trust. The boys found the cycles ideal to plough through the muddy moor pathways and country roads. The bike was heavy and wonderful when freewheeling downhill, but cycling uphill was another matter. Nevertheless the boys enjoyed the freedom and exercise.

Their printed stories were mostly about farm life and livestock. An outbreak of some contagious disease and its consequences would be front page news and likely to be discussed at length in the local public house. A real scandal was hard to find in this quiet country area but when found made a good blowout of all the old rumours and usually let out in daily episodes. One day of the blue a rumour that a farm labourer had been murdered nearby. It had been rumoured it had been a fight about a woman. Two of the three men lifting potatoes on a hill farm had fell out in a jealous rage and one had punched the other who had retaliated by picked up a stone and struck the other on the head. The blow had opened the man's scull and proved sufficient to kill him. Sergeant Brown was a tall elderly grey haired man who knew the district well. He also knew that to capture the murderer he would have to check each farm yard and the derelict railway tunnels situated a mile from the old Saw Mill. The land was fairly open with the exception of the young pine forests. So with the limited manpower available he had to single out the priorities. The sergeant guessed there was more to the killing than for the favours of a woman. He knew also that gambling was the favourite pastime of the labourers and had one of his constables placed undercover in the village betting shop. About two weeks later in the afternoon the farm worker who had committed the offence turned to place a bet only to be met by the constable. He at once admitted self-defence explaining how they had bet on a horse and another prize of a woman both had feelings for. The labourers only knew the other man as Max. But he admitted the man was so evasive it was impossible to tell if that were true. "One thing I'm sure of he was German and as you British would say arrogant with it. Naturally he won the bet and rubbed it whenever he had the chance. Each night in the Willow Tree restaurant he would deliberately kiss her continuously with one eye on me. At first it was acceptable but as time went by a thorn prick grew into a sabre cut and thoughts of revenge crept silently into my soul. On the hill where the wind blew partial rain into our eyes and sore muscles reminded us it was near finishing time. Karl began his clowning and telling me of his oncoming passionate night. That was the straw that broke the camel's back. I picked up the biggest stone I could find and threw it at him. I saw his head bounce to the right with such force I knew he was a goner. I had done for the German bastard, no regrets."

The sergeant allowed Cameron and Geordie to cover and print the story. But told Cameron there may have been a conspiracy with some of the other farm workers, a few of them had come from the continent to avoid conscription. Later that day a hollow tree trunk was found to be a hiding place for gambling money. It was a place where they could throw the money into if surprised by the police. It had contained over twenty pounds of half-crowns left in a panic. Sergeant Brown wondered if the money found had something to do with the murder other than the bet, yet the criminal door was open to many other theories. Geordie and Cameron were inclined to see the incident as a straight forward killing in a jealous rage. As far as they were concerned they had a story that made them feel like New York Pressmen in a James Stewart movie, now they had become real men of the news world.

3.
Comfort before Honour.

It was one of those bright Sundays where the sun's rays filled the dining room giving an air of a bright optimistic day. There was the lingering odour of a hot breakfast as Geordie, Larry, Robert, Molina, Cameron and his parents sat on the stout wooden chairs listening to the BBC News while sipping tea. As each item of news came up they would debate its worth and effect on the people of the county. Sundays broadcast was mainly of the benefits of tinned food interspersed with a warning of an announcement by the PM Mr Chamberlain at 11.15.am.

Opinions and laughter drowned out most of the PM's announcement till they heard the astounding words, "This country is at war with Germany. Now may God bless you all. May He defend the right. We shall be fighting against, brute force, bad faith, injustice, oppression and persecution and then I am certain that the right will prevail." Cameron noticed the party mood still prevailed as if that broadcast had never happened, as if to say why it should interrupt the fun. But it was inevitable that someone would come to their senses and tell them the party is over. Cameron stood up and looked at his father puffing at his black pipe completely content with his life. His father was about to get up from his chair when he began to wonder at the expression on his sons face. "What is it this time?" he seemed a bit impatient. Then he was as quick to apologise for his ill manners, as it was very unlike him to be so sharp. Cameron said after gathering his thoughts, "Hitler and his cohorts are now at war with us; we all saw it coming but didn't want to believe it. I wonder what people are now thinking of those in the Labour party that had not opposed Fascism but also deterred rearmament by causing trouble in the factories. We can't lie down to this, can we dad? David sighed again, "No sane person would want a repeat of the last war. Just look around and you will see people are walking around as normal just doing their jobs and looking after their families. We are beginning to get back on our feet after a war and multiple banking problems. Would they rather sit in a wet ditch with a gasmask on waiting for the gas clouds to appear, I doubt it. Or advance into a hail of ball bearings from German eighteen pounders. I was with the French at the beginning of the war when they wore red trousers and blue jackets. I saw country boys walk into hails of hellish machinegun fire. And rows of them lying side by side cut down like grass under the autumn skies when they should have been at home with their girlfriends." David then sang part of a Robert Burns song.

> When wild war's deadly blast was blown,
> And gentle Peace returning.
> With many a sweet babe fatherless,
> And many a widow mourning,
> I left the lines and tented field,
> Where long I'd been a lodger;
> My humble knapsack a' my wealth,
> a poor and honest soldier.

"I saw the brave soldiers in Flanders and like me they dreamt of the day they would be on their way home and thought of this song, but never expected it all to happen again. All I can say is I'm sorry that it has come to this; we should have stood up to them. One other thing, both parliamentary parties were as bad as each other. Did you know that when Chamberlain went to the Parliament with his letter promising peace in our time only one MP advocated war and that was Conservative Duff Cooper? His resignation over the Munich Agreement was described as, "the first step in the road back to national sanity. But there were no other steps till it was far too late." Now other sons and daughters will pay dearly."

Cameron's Mother recognising the seriousness of the remarks rose from the table and opened a bottle of good whisky and gave them all a stiff drink. There could not have been a better time to sip the water of life, and let the golden liquid slowly bring the sensation of warmth, Geordie thought, as his teeth bit involuntarily into the glass. War had been a million miles from his mind that morning as he was certain of his future with the newspaper as snow on the hills in winter. He was sure nothing would stand in the way of his chosen path. David left the unanswered questions in the air. It was the best place for them as they sipped the welcome whisky.

A few glasses more and they were ready to have a party, pushing the war news out of their lives. They were young and full of life and soon put the table and chairs aside to dance and sing. Cameron and Molina danced to 'Oh, I'll never go out with Riley anymore.' Cameron had to admit to himself he have been in love with Molina for a long time and now with the news of another conflict he wanted to tell her, but he was sure Larry was her kind of guy. Still he edged towards her and followed her closely from room to room and chair to chair. He did this well into the evening. Sometimes Molina would stop and look at him strangely and shrug her shoulders.

Geordie put a black comb under his nose and did a good Hitler imitation while Robert did the goose step kicking Geordie up the backside. Molina gave a breath-taking Can Can showing her lovely long legs. Cameron's father David gave them a pleasant rendition of 'Ye banks and Braes O Bonny Doon.' The tune somehow seemed so significant at the time and made Cameron's insides take a tumble. It was not only for the song but thought that all their futures were now at risk because of a madman who had obtained ultimate power in Germany and wanted more. The sky was now losing its blue tint, filtering in dark purple that allowed stars to slowly fill the heavens. The stars were like invited guests bringing the gift of companionship to this uncertain world. Cameron and Molina wanted some fresh air and walked along a path that followed a shallow stream that reflected the brighter stars. Molina asked Cameron why he had been following her. Cameron could only blurt out self-consciously, "sorry Molina I didn't realise what I was doing it surely must have been the whisky." The opportunity he had prayed for in the kitchen had arisen and Cameron had stupidly messed it up and could not think of a word to say that might recapture the moment as they walked back to the cottage.

To Cameron father the years between the wars despite the hardships were ones of hope; the long nights of the Great War fast falling behind them. There had been some political doubts to the power of the Versailles Treaty. But since 1924 the treaty had been all but ignored, yet Hitler had repeated the humiliation over and over so that its fading power still stung the nerves of Germans. On the other side it was thought that the German people had learned their lesson. To police the treaty as part of the new world plans the League of Nations was determined to step in if trouble arose. With its combined forces it was certain to deter an attack by an outsider or on any of the other treaty signatories. There was still lingering suspicions that haunted the population despite the men of goodwill like Chamberlain, Stresemann and Briand who laboured for a sound peace. Resentment had remained in Germany and sustained by being taught like a religion. In parallel there was a continuous nagging fear in France the German problem was still there. These were some of the properties that allowed the lunatics to grow in strength.

4.

Great Liars are also Great Magicians.

Seven years before the rise of Hitler to become the German Fuhrer Italy had produced their version of Fascism, a strutting devil named Mussolini who would soon to become Hitler's faithful 'jackal.' What a predicament we had allowed ourselves to get into. Cameron thought it seemed impossible to do the right thing; there was always another fatal blow to follow. When the Abyssinian (Ethiopia) crisis arose Britain and France backed the defence of that country, only to find by their positive action they had pushed Italy into the arms of Germany. Britain was not without blame as when the Anglo-German naval agreement allowed Herr Hitler to increase his naval and air forces. Cameron was sure that the world did not need another powerful competitive navy. To make matters worse the agreement was done without consulting France its main ally. France then in turn snuggled up to El Duce Benito Mussolini, Founder of the Empire. Each had their own opinion and freely to express them. Larry had fallen out with Cameron about the backstairs diplomacy of the British and French Hoare-Laval Pact being signed in secret offering Mussolini large chunks of Abyssinia Including parts of that country still unconquered. Leaving what was left of Abyssinia with a corridor to the sea named 'a corridor for camels'. Robert did not disagree on all the points as P.M. Baldwin had ended the pact having it signed by his Foreign Secretary on December date four years ago. But Molina argued this squabble allowed Italy to attack Abyssinia and take it all by the use of modern weapons against tribesmen. Larry thought rightly that this incident ended the hopes of the League of Nations but at the same time argued the pact was the right thing to do. A host of nations left including Spain, Sweden, Norway, and Finland. While the Germany of the 1920s had changed and was now with a new found bravado clambering for Lebensraum and proclaiming itself as the defence of the west against the Red Peril (Russia). Robert had believed the Red Peril and was sympathetic to the German people even when Hitler sent his men to murder the Austrian Chancellor. Molina had been busy training as a doctor and had missed most of the changing face of Europe. Germany was in a fever to rearm and showed the weakness of democratic countries by marching into the Rhineland. Still Robert gave Hitler the benefit of the doubt especially when Lord Lothian said Hitler 'had only walked into his own back-garden.' Amid German promises of a 25 year none aggression pact the French Popular Front was elected and promised social reform rather than action. This convinced him that the world was changing for the better. Geordie was the only one to see that the mirror of Hitler had no soul when he marched into an Austria. A Country that had clearly been blackmailed into being swallowed into Hitler's growing empire. Geordie could see the next shameful event transpire when the valuable outpost of Czechoslovakia was next on the list. He had realised that the democratic nation's honour had been on trial for their lives while they had been sleeping.

The British wanted peace and quiet and to have this you had to keep out of trouble. There was no doubt the standard of living in Britain was slowly rising allowing people to buy more luxury goods, but at what price. Geordie knew the British still looked on the continentals as being amusing, amiable and most important as harmless. The world knew we had respected the two very British players, Baldwin with his pipe and Chamberlain with his umbrella both symbols of steadfastness and confident security. Surely no one could deny that.

5.

Hitler may never have been a Gentleman at all.

When daylight came the following morning the gang were still weary from the night before. Still they had the appetite of the young, enough to eat one of Cameron's mother's hearty breakfasts. Through the meal they explored what would be their chosen course in a changed world that had closed some doors and opened others.

Geordie and Cameron were now being sent to London to train as War Correspondents a far cry from a local rag reporter. They were full of themselves brimming with confidence and that the future would be just as full of excitements. Cameron knew he would miss his friends but there was one nagging worry and that was Robert. Robert had told him he had changed his view on Hitler and yet he and his family were still quite friendly with some people in Germany. There was in Britain plenty of evident warmth and feelings of kinship with the blond haired and blue eyed Germans that had existed since the 1930s and not just royalty but in businesses. Robert had mentioned that his family had agreed Herr Hitler was an unusual choice, but the people of Germany seemed delighted with him. All of Europe had to acknowledge that he had brought some sense of order to the region. Compared to France, Germany was growing and confident while 'Belle France' was more like a banana republic changing governments more often than not. To Roberts family undesirable news reported from Germany was just European behaviour and was expected of them. After all they were a different nation and had separate views and notions. More importantly, any uncomfortable news from Germany was often seen as an exaggeration. It had been reported in

14

1922 that during a Hitler speech he was seen with a halo over his head and was believed my many as a sign from god.

Chamberlain in the heat of appeasement had returned from Munich waving his piece of Paper at Heston airport to cheering crowds delivered the 'I believe it is peace in our time,' speech. There were crowds to meet him at 10 Downing St. All of them apparently blind to the bitter truth that seems to have escaped them as they busied themselves in daily life. Hitler inevitably broke his word and was now not considered to be a gentleman and just as amazing he may never have been one in the first place.

It had been a great puzzle to Cameron when heard that the Poland had been on Germany's side at Munich and happily took a chunk out of Czechoslovakia. Poland had then signed a (none aggression pact) with Germany. Ribbentrop a master at foreign affairs wanted to make a deal with Poland for the Polish Corridor that separated West and Eastern Prussia. He knew in the long run Poland needed the trade across the corridor to ensure its reliance on Germany. It was possible that he could bribe Poland with some land in the Ukraine as compensation sometime in the future. But Herr Hitler decided he could not wait and defiantly attacked Poland. Despite Hitler's instincts it did not work out according to his time table, due to Polish delays and other events forcing his hand. The British government signed a unilateral guarantee to Poland against German aggression at the end of March. Hitler had told his unsure army to hold back on the polish problem, but the very next day the Polish ambassador passed a note rejecting the deal on the corridor. The Polish army newspaper proudly announced they would not be browbeaten and that victory would certainly be theirs in a case of war. The polish people believed in a victory and expected to fight as they always had.

Cameron had news from the battlefields of a new type of warfare unleashed on Poland. The use of the radio, tanks, aircraft and fast moving artillery and infantry changed warfare forever. Cameron knew the Military chiefs in Britain, Poland and France still exalted the virtues of cavalry up to near two years before the attack on Poland. Some even though tanks and aircraft were only accessories to the man and horse. The top brass in Britain in 1937 were suspicions of those who advocated mechanised warfare calling them 'tank-maniacs.' Britain eventually created a rag and bone armoured division in Egypt but it was not until May of 1939 that the decision was made to have one at home, this was despite having the best man in the tank business Basil Liddell Hart at hand in England.

6.

The Place where Love Resides.

Larry our hero athlete wanted to become a Padre in the Armed Forces. He had studied Theology at University and chased all the girls at prayer meetings just to keep his hand in. Where there were pretty girls at a prayer meeting Larry would be with them singing his heart out. Both the love of God and the love of women went hand in hand. He explained it this way, "Love of God opens the door to love everything and who better to love than young adorable women." "I must admit you have excellent love logic, whether it is from the old or New Testament who cares," Cameron agreed. He had not been surprised when the news of him joining the Royal Navy as a Padre reached them later. On board ship he would have it easy with a captive audience and in each port a potential captivated girl.

Molina had joined her father's practice driving daily to help the farmers and villagers over the moor hills. She seemed to have put her opinions of Larry and Cameron aside to engage in her profession. Her help was vital and had its rewards in keeping the sparse population healthy, but life on the moors was never smooth there was always some incident that would spark loose talk. So it was imperative for her to be seen as saintly but at the same time rightly human. She liked a drink in the local public house and willingly joined in the banter. One night she heard a rough voice shout, "Have you noticed that women are now in every profession and pretend to be as good as a man?" Walter from the piggery had shouted over the noise as Molina settled at the bar. Molina was quick to reply. "You see your pigs every day and considered the rest of the world to be like them. But you see men are restless animals while woman are the home makers.

In other words they are the makers of civilisation and therefore the whole world. Whilst you are the maker of bacon a good breakfast food." Some of the men cheered as others turned their back on the conversation and others mumbled as their words in time became lost in the chatter. Molina lived in a village of twelve houses situated along the single lonely road. She had flowers gracing the front wall and vines on the cottage sides and an extensive back lawn surrounded by a green fence. Molina thought her cottage was taken from a movie where Ronald Coleman lived. She had the only car in the village which was an old battered Ford that started with a series of minor explosions. The car according to the village occupants was better than any alarm clock to waken them early in the morning. As the car ran down the village street it fired off grey balls of exhaust fumes amid loud bangs that also awakened four local dogs that would pursuit the car. They would race in the excitement, but as the car reached a row of trees at the edge of the village the dogs lay down with exhaustion. Her car was named 'Miss Obsolete' by the motor mechanic who had to search far and wide for spare parts. The inside of her cottage was traditional and comfortable. Her favourite piano was placed opposite the broad fire place. The cottage was a constant meeting place for her friends who liked to sit by the glow of her fire. Molina would make coffee and accompanied by homemade biscuits. As it usually rained regularly throughout the spring, summer and autumn months there was nowhere more comfortable than Molina's fire place. Outside may have been green and lush or have snow and sun but Molina's cottage was the byword for comfort.

7.

Of all the Farewells he had ever known.

Cameron thought of her as he and Geordie sat in a cold rail carriage he could imagine the warmth of Molina fireplace and felt a sense of loss. He would think of the warmth of her smiling lips and wished he had taken advantage of the opportunity he let float away so pathetically on the river bank. In the Edinburgh Waverley station Cameron stood by the inside carriage door holding the window leather strap tightly. Molina waved gently, her green eyes dewy and her lips puckered in the form of a kiss. Another kiss he wished he had taken there and then, all he had to do was run out onto the platform, but he could not bring himself to do so. The station was a mass of noises, paperboys shouting at the top of their voices over the loud hiss of steam from the huge engines. The loud speaker's mumbled senseless information that made travellers look up at the speakers as if the messages were in a foreign language. The whistle blew for departure and the Guard waved his green lamp as a belt of white steam drifted over Molina. She appeared to vanish, lost in a crowd as the train moved grudgingly along the platform. The noises and the speed rush became blanked out by the sudden darkness as the train ran into the tunnel. Geordie had the impression he leaving his past behind and he could never go back to the same place he had just left seconds ago. Their train was full of men in uniform Geordie noticed in the window reflections against the dark tunnel. He saw men caught in a frame of contagious laughter while others sat in a silent vigil. He wondered if they were remembering what they had just left behind were now questioning providence if they would ever return again.

8.

The Lightening War.

Germany's blitzkrieg against Poland had been launched by two army groups supported by a massive air offensive that destroyed Poland's air force in two days. Within eight days they were on the outskirts of Warsaw. General Kutrzeba bravely counter attacked, but on the 19th September the Battle of the Bzura was over. The day before on the 18th September as the German pincer closed near Brest-Litovsk the Russians crossed the eastern frontier. The then polish government fled to Rumania while Warsaw held out to the 27th September. Russia and Germany now shared a broken country, the Germans hastily taking most of the manufacturing areas.

Robert was at home as the first star appeared over the windswept moorland. He was relaxing while reading the letters from his German friends; he found them interesting especially their opinions on the sinking of the Graf Spree. Germany had known they could not match the Royal Navy in a surface war but a new idea of using submarines and powerful fast pocket battleships would cut the British lifelines ending her maritime capabilities in commerce. The Graf Spree had left her harbour before the war began hoping for instant results. On September 29th she was in the South Atlantic in the waiting area before moving west. Her fist victim was the British vessel 'Clement.' The captain of the Clement followed instructions burning her papers and sending out radio messages ignoring radio silence allowing them time to get rid of the ships information and damaging the engines and then the radio. In answer to this Captain Langsdorff thought it was better to sneak up on his victims before they could follow their procedures. From the South Atlantic to the Indian Ocean the Graf

Spree was the ideal marauder of the sea lanes. On the night of the 12th and 13th December while patrolling on the River Plate the sighting of two masts on the distant horizon was reported to the captain. Langsdorff ordered his ship to turn in the direction of the two masts on the morning with prospects for a bit of target practice. But what he had seen were HMS Exeter and two ships of the Achilles class, instead of firing practice he had to run for his life in the River Plate.

It ended with the Graf Spree being scuttled on the estuary of the river plate close to neutral Montevideo on the 17th December. The German propaganda machine went quickly into action. Their overeager report told of how the Graf Spree had sunk a heavy cruiser and damaged two light cruisers while she had been only slightly damaged. But they had found it difficult later to explain the embarrassment of a great armoured ship destroyed by her own crew. Contrary to this the Battle of the river Plate in Britain was a major sea victory that added to the reputation of the First Lord of the Admiralty Winston Churchill. Whereas Hitler had no real faith in battleships and the events of Montevideo confirmed this. Unfortunately submarines then became one of his pet ideas. Robert felt that it had been a lucky break for the British which turned to her disadvantage as submarine warfare began in earnest. Robert realised once again he was uncertain of his alliances.

He knew that British and German views differed on Hitler whom both had deemed as having some attributes of greatness but seemed to be wanting in normal human qualities. Out of the games of history there comes a certain man caught in the circumstances of his time, the combination is an explosion of events totally unexpected. Hitler was seen as a jumped up corporal to the German High Command and almost laughable. His speedy rise was beyond their belief and to become their supreme commander from corporal was unthinkable. Then in time they the high command were his subordinates having to swear allegiance to him and fight as ordered. Most of the diplomats considered this upstart as low and raw in want of skill. But before long he outflanked them and double crossed them and beat them at their best. German industrialists knew he looked and acted as a clown but they too were forced to toe the line. He would not listen to advice he was expected to adhere to instead relying on his own instincts. But these instincts that appeared common and rash had brought him to his destiny at lightning speed. It soon became difficult to criticise him following them. As a school boy his master noted a lack of discipline and being cantankerous, arrogant and hostile to advice. After the Great War he had lived in Vienna in a hand to mouth existence, neither drinking nor smoking nor chasing the girls. Some found this to be strange even unnatural. His attempts at art were unsuccessful and his natural indolence forbade him from applying himself to any exertion and from this failure he drifted into politics. He practised oratory and gestures which compelled the listener with his compulsive talk, mesmerising his audience awakening their imagination. Adolf Hitler they said walked into a room sniffed the air for a moment groping and feeling his way to senses the atmosphere and his audience. His words like an arrow would hit the target. Goring would later say, "The conviction was spoken, word for word, as if from my own soul." Hitler's great energy came from his hideous ego and his belief he was a man of destiny as great as a Nordic Caesar. To the German nation he was the new Messiah. Beyond the image he created was an unreliable man almost without morals. He was unsound and monstrous believing in only himself and his chosen destiny. One of Robert's friends wrote it would be foolish to deny his greatness coming from obscurity to power within a few years to fulfil the national craving of millions of Germans who had no purpose in their lives. Robert thought of those 'no purpose, no purpose in their lives.' The leader had filled the vacuum in their lives with his heady words and made the Army swear alliance to him. Then abolished the high unemployment of what may be called the cast outs and probably most important of all fed their self-esteem. For those meagre advantages he took away their hard won civil rights and gave himself ultimate power over them. His road to power was carefully done under the law. He had the wit and patience to hold back to the right time by the use of his careful calculations. Adolf Hitler's genius was also in the men to help him on his rise to power. They were diverse which suited his plan, such as the appointed Goebbels a speculator from working class routes. Goring the well-known air ace who in August of 1939 promised the Ruhr will not be subjected to a single bomb. Goring was the most outstanding of Hitler's underlings and the only one with upper-class claims of aristocracy. He was also primarily the founder of the Gestapo the secret police of Nazi Germany. Heinrich Himmler SS number 168. He opened his first concentration camp at Dachau in 1933. Also, he was the architect of Operation Himmler creating the impression of Polish hostility to justify the invasion of Poland. All threw their hats in the ring and followed blindly under Hitler's spell giving the Nazi's that scrupulous dynamic. Bizarrely his followers who would follow him into a nightmare knew that Hitler was not German by birth. But, what was truly apparent by the 1930s Germany created a primitive terror in her neighbours that took the rest of the world some time to realise. Barbara Tuchman wrote, "The world became aware of the beast beneath the German skin."

9.

Dark days in London.

Cameron and Geordie arrived in London late at night and were surprised to find it buzzing with life. The first sign of a Londoner were three firemen running in a kind of shuffle adorned in canvass Gasmasks which made Cameron shrink in horror; this was his first introduction to a civilian war. At the London Daily Express they were introduced to Alan Moorhead a real writer known throughout the business and worthily praised. Alan had that look of a cheerful fellow about to laugh at any time. They knew they were total amateurs and ready to fall at his feet. Instead Alan made friends with them which helped win over the other reporters. Their first night around town was a visit to a musical show at the London Palladium called 'The Little Dog Laughed' with the Crazy Gang the main performers. Even the blackout could not prevent the West Enders from enjoying themselves, possessing that free spirit to enjoy the shows of London. The Sherman Fisher Girls were a big hit with Geordie in particular and without exaggeration wildly appreciated by all the men in the audience. In the dark lit theatre Cameron could just make out the features and faces of the audience. Some of the girls with upward faces looked like angels reminding him of Molina when she was in her teens and full of an angels grace. His heart beat faster and longed to see her again, the time away had given him the opportunity to examine his true feelings. But there was so much to see and hear in the capital so that he had less opportunity to mope. Gracie Fields had recovered from the long illness and was singing on the BBC radio and for those craving some culture The Old Vic Company played St Joan at Streatham Hill. The main part was played by Constance

Cummings who was a famous film star. She had been a favourite of Cameron since her last three pictures 'Remember Last Night, Seven Sinners and Strangers on Honeymoon.'

Cameron thought he would never have made a good soldier, which at first upset him, but as a reporter or war correspondent he felt he could contribute to the war effort. And yet he was now comfortable in a uniform with the exception of his battle dress trousers which were somewhat baggy. Anyway he noticed nearly everyone else's uniform was too large or too tight. Geordie's battledress blouse sleeves went far passes his hands and his hat covered his ears. Thankfully they had access to a good tailor who remedied their uniforms ill fittings which was more than could be said for many a soldier marching around London like one of the crazy gang.

The training was very basic. Cameron and Geordie both recognised small weapon training was of vital importance. Both favoured pistol practice as it gave the impression the war would be more like a romantic cowboy movie. But the reality was far removed as hardly a night passed without some bad news. On a night in October the Royal Oak was sunk at the loss of near 833 lives, the news was broadcast early on a Sunday morning when much of population was sound asleep. The great ship had fought in Jutland and would have been considered obsolete had it not been for the coming war. Captain W.G. Benn had survived. An 18 year old boy survived by stripping off his cloths and tying his life belt around his waist then jumped into the oily sea. Two of his friends swam for a time with him but disappeared forever on the mile and a half swim to the shore cliffs. The cliffs were around 30 foot high which must have been daunting after a long cold swim. Every person Geordie and Cameron met was shocked and dismayed at the ease the great ship had been sunk, and the great loss of life. So this is the real thing Cameron thought, so many lives lost in the dark night by thunderous explosions and fire. The only alternative was the bitter night oily seas. And while all this was happening London the greatest target in the world was left untouched.

The British troops had landed in France several weeks before. The first British Expeditionary Force known as the Contemptibles of 1939 were on the way to the front. Lord Gort was the General under French command bringing back memories of the Great War. General Gort was given the right to appeal to the British Cabinet when the circumstances became necessary. But in the middle of a battle there was little time to haggle, that point had not been considered properly if at all. Trains ran miraculously on time day and night from all over Britain. They culminated at the furiously busy dockyards. All kinds of troop ships waited to sail to France where the troops would receive a rousing reception from the locals. It was reported and held that the magnificent Maginot Line allowed for the safety of the troops to reach the front. "That must be so or at least I hope so" agreed Geordie "We must go and see it sometime after a spot of leave." Cameron approved as his thoughts returned to his week of leave and a visit to see Molina once more.

He was drinking on the train which he had never been keen on. A fellow traveller dressed for a night at the opera leaned over and asked in a northern accent, "I'm a not too bad judge of character young man and can see you have the expression of someone in consternation. I suspect it is something personal. Am I correct lad?" Cameron had that lonely melancholy feeling travels are often struck by, especially during night travel. The stranger looked and sounded so amiable he was happy to talk for a while. After all it's unlikely he would ever see that man again. This feeling was now powerful and had begun to change his views. Instead of hello world, it was now more a goodbye.

10.

Failure is a Stranger in his Own House.

He began by telling the stranger of a day when he was a young boy sitting by the road side in a warm summer. It was a single road that wound down from the hill side, a solitary place where wild life was free to roam free from harm. He had just left his grandmothers cottage and under his arm he held a parcel of comic books and cakes. Above the sound of Sky Larks and Lapwing he could hear a faint crying sound. He looked towards the sound to see a young girl weeping in the tall grass verge. Cameron had little to do with girls at that time and was more than curious but cautious. "What can so bad to make you cry on a beautiful morning like this?" The girl had lost her golden retriever. Her dog Toby had run away chasing after a flock of starlings that in a panic and had flown uphill towards a dark woodland. Cameron hoping the dog was lost in the corn. He raced uphill pushing the corn aside with his arms while his feet stamped the rough ground. Someway up the hill near the line of trees he saw the dog jumping in the air trying to fly. It ran and jumped as high as it could but soon to fell to the ground with a thud. It took some time for Cameron to entice Toby to follow him, but his persistence eventually paid. He proudly brought Toby back to Molina who rewarded him with a faint kiss on the cheek. He was so overawed by Molina's friendliness he gave her his parcel and ran off, down the road toward the town. Cameron had not thought of love with the exception of the beautiful Greta Garbo he saw in a movie. Her fair face had been like a Madonna wrapped in warm fur as the snowflakes fell on her full lips. Molina was real and not an image on a screen and to prove it she had kissed him. That night sleep wouldn't come as mixtures of love saddened and elated him in turn. One thing he was sure of was this feeling of being alive was brand new and he wanted to keep it in his heart always. He truly expected to marry Molina and had never lost that feeling despite the things that happened. At school he protected her and had a few black eyes and skinned knees to prove it, but it was worth it. Molina and Cameron soon became fast friends not only in school but in everyday activities. He could not tell her how he really felt in a million years. But for all stars in the universe he would not change his feelings.

He told the stranger she had not replied to his recent letters emphasising they were not love letters. "That may be the heart of the problem my man." Adjusting his large white tie the man winked and said, "If you truly feel for that young woman get off your backside, there is a war and a romance to win. How lucky you are, but remember she will not wait forever. What if someone beats you to her heart? Then you may pay the price of a lonely life which is a common misery." Cameron was beginning to feel sleepy but managed a nod in agreement before drifting off. He had no wish to be rude to the stranger but needs must. He slipped into a dream that was dramatically interrupted by the flashes of bright lights as the train passed stations and then sank into the darkness of the countryside. When Cameron awoke the stranger was gone but he remembered his warning, all he had to ask himself was Molina worth fighting for and an unquestionable answer was 'Yes.'

11.

Life will Love you back.

Molina was at work attending to patients with her father in the small practice whose headquarters were in a renovated country school. She was happy to follow in Thomas her fathers footsteps, his reputation for kindness and understanding was legendary. But his years training as a doctor had not been easy as he lived in a time of strife and uncertainty. The 1929 crash wiped out all his savings and like many of his friends the crash left him in serious debt that took years to pay. A few years later his attractive wife Diana who had been a nurse in his training hospital left him for an Egyptian air pilot. Mohammad the pilot had been blessed with plenty of money and easy charm but a little careless. He injured himself while drinking Spanish brandy climbing a tree and shouting insults to passer-by's, a branch snapped and down went the pilot on to a hard ground. It was during his time as a patient he met Diana and swept her off her feet. She left with him leaving a note apologising for the haste and that was the last time he saw evidence of the existence of his wife Diana. Molina had not long begun school at went into her mother's room hoping to find some clue or memory looking under the bed and sliding between the layers of bed linen. One day she saw a silk handkerchief that had belonged to her mother, lifted it to her nose expecting to smell her mother's scent, instead found the hankie odourless and bland. Molina realised like the scent her mother had gone for good. Two years that time and could not understand why her mother had left her. She often later it was reported the pilot had crashed his plane somewhere in the Amazon jungle and was never found again, despite the months of extensive searches. Diana never so much as sent a word to them of regret or mentioned her fears it was possible she had already found a substitute for the lost pilot. This made it more difficult to close that chapter in the lives of both Molina and her father. It took time and each month and year of appreciable distance lessened the hurt. Her father began to recognise the value of his talented daughter and her insatiable thirst for knowledge. She had in fact become his inspiration. To Molina her success and her father's determination were as important as the blood that flowed through her veins. Work and more work formed a set pattern advancing her towards her eventual goal of becoming a doctor. Now with a war beginning she had decided there would be little time for romance as her skills as a doctor would be needed. She knew Cameron had looked at her differently lately, which she found strange and bewildering. It seemed to Molina in one instant she had been caught in a shy mode and then in a bewildering magic moment of emotion. When they were near to each other time appeared to stand still and a sense of well-being swept over her and did wonder felt the same. But she had to shrug the feelings off before they could go further. She quickly returned to the reality of being a doctor and owing her alliances to her country patients.

12.

Coming Home makes the World Richer.

Waverley station was as busy as ever when Cameron detrained, the now familiar noises were a welcome home to him as he gathered his leather suitcases. While around the steam and hurried movement of travellers evaporated within minutes leaving an empty platform. A porter appeared and took Cameron's bags placing them on a trolley without so much as speaking a word. The porter pulled back his shoulders, pretending to be an ex-soldier, stood to attention and saluted before moving quickly on to the taxi rank. He knew in this war climate he was sure to get a handsome tip if he was thought to be someone with a military past. Cameron in his uniform with his short haircut and shiny shoes marched behind amused at the antics of the porter. The porter was delighted to received half a crown which he rubbed against his trouser leg to shine it up. Dropped it into his pocket and marched off happily whistling the British Grenadiers.

The black haired taxi driver was cheery and talkative asking all sorts of questions about London night life. He centred on the fatal dangers of the blackout and the Russian invasion of Finland where he had come from some years before. Cameron had heard through correspondent channels five Russian divisions had crossed into Finland. They were bogged down in the deepening snow and easy targets for the skiing Fins. Both the taxi driver and Cameron talked of the fear the Russians must have endured being cut off in sub-zero temperatures in the wild forests and being hunted down by white camouflaged soldiers. From the taxi window Cameron looked at the Lothian hills rolling by with patches of heather and gullies of bog resting in long reeds. He felt comforted being home safe for the world that was now going crazier by the day and had no one to stop it. Cameron thought that in the future some writers would make a fortune out of how we could have avoided this conflict like the last one and the one before. Every one of them a singular fool bathing themselves in their own monumental conceit. The bus depot was in turmoil with soldiers chatting and smoking. Kitbags were in piles crisscrossing the pavements making it difficult to negotiate a way around them. Cameron recognised Jimmy MacDougal's red lined bus and his wife Aggie the conductress near the end of the line. Their bus parked well askew for the others. She spotted Cameron and ran to him, hugged the breath out of his lungs and kissed his burning cheeks. "Your home from the wars, are you not my bonny lad?" She shouted over the noise of chattering bus engines. Slapping him on the back and pushing aside soldiers preoccupied in conversations in her path as she led him to her bus. In the bus that was warm and clean she made a short speech to those on-board that Cameron was sure could be heard a few miles away. "Our local newspaper man Cameron has returned from London that foreign country where the Queen God lives in a muckle great house called Bucking harm Castle. The trains run under the ground like worms and come up at Kings Cross where the king must live. I have to say for country a lass it doesn't seem natural to me." "Away you go Aggie give the lad a chance to sit and rest awhile." Jimmy MacDougal intervened as he put his bus in gear with an accompanying long screech. Along the way Aggie sang in a soft tone one of her journeying favourites. 'Auld Scots Mother Mine.' Soon the passengers joined in while drifting into their own memories mother and of home. Cameron thought what the hell and put his shyness to the side and joined in full heartedly. Mind you he thought of the granny on his mother's side who was American and had married a Scot whose grandfather was suspected of being Spanish. On my Father's side the Scots blood ran to the Jacobean times and beyond always willing to fight in any side that produced a sack of two of gold. But the words were full of nostalgia and were strong in memories of times long gone. The stories told by his father intermingled with his own creating a show of a friendly fire place where the family sat around in blissful contentment.

The hills far on the moorland had small patches of November snow. The sheep clung to the precarious slops of hills looking down at those passing with disinterest. One of the ewe's with her lamb on her back climbed an edge that would have challenged many a hill climber. The sheep were at home in the high solitude where the north easterly winds brought snow early. The weather made life harsh and cold for the birds that flew in the currents and the ground hard for hares and rabbits. Looking closer he saw the sheep had made distinguishable paths twisting around the hill sides that must have taken decades to make. A lone hawk spun over dense pine trees that sheltered some of the moorland animals. Following the glen a river widened and narrowed in others both great place for the fishing especially where a wooden bridge rested near the village Inn. Old churches surrounded by pine and wild flowers dominated the quiet village cottages their standing reminded the cottage dwellers of their linked past. Jimmies bus came to a halt not far from Molina's cottage pumping exhaust fumes into the clear air. Its engine swayed and thumped as the bus emptied its cargo of hardened country folk. During an emotional farewell from Aggie, Cameron listened to her news of the territorial's leaving the villages behind the pipe bands and as the sounds drifted away all that was left was lonely places for the mothers, fathers and young girls.

In Molina's cottage a handsome big fire burned and crackled cheerfully. Her father Thomas Mason was first to shake Cameron's hand and wish him well. Molina hugged him and kissed him timidly on the cheek. Much to his surprise Larry was there looking good in his Padre uniform with a confident smile on his face. Larry shook his hand and slapped his back offering him a glass of golden whisky. Cameron noticed the table was full of drinks and good food, knowing that a close friendship with the butcher and the famers paid and was the country way. He was ushered to a seat next to the fire and told to eat well. After the table was cleared away Larry said he had an important announcement to make. Cameron could not contain the beating of his heart and nearly fell over. "I'm on my way in two days' time to the fleet to teach the heathen matelots the word of god and to respect all men including the Pongo's." Larry would be that man to do just that, Cameron thought. Larry our boxing champion and hard rugger man was a towering man of action and with his love of people he would surely be an excellent Padre to the men. The last of the light came through a window and before fading brought a new moon that spread its haunting Silver light over the lawn. Molina was near the window gazing out while deep in her thoughts. She looked like a moon goddess in some fairy-tale ready to leave this bunging world of fools and fly to a silvery paradise. While Cameron was still getting over the shock of Larry's announcement for he was sure it would be the engagement of Molina and him. Reaching over Cameron took her hand and asked how her practice was faring. "Much the same as it has always been every call is an emergency until it's time to pay the bill." Just then the phone rang and Thomas who was standing next to it picked it up at the same time looking towards shrugging his shoulders. "Molina I must go, one of the moorland farmers is in need of medical assistance, I hope he has a ready bottle in the house when I arrive." His laughter rang along the lobby until he closed the door. Molina switched on the lights and the room became colourful and warm. They talked into the night as old friends reliving their past. Cameron relayed his fond memory of Molina the tomboy in her dungarees covered in mud climbing a tree and not being able to climb down. The boys formed a net with their arms and told her to jump down. This she did and knocked out Geordie's front tooth and bled Robert's nose while kicking Cameron's shin. They agreed that if this should happen again Molina would have stay in the tree and wait for the fire brigade. Larry and Cameron shared a room until Larry began snoring enough to scare the devil. Much as Cameron tried to bury his head in the pillows he could not stop the continuous tortuous assault on his ears. He took his blankets and pillows to the sofa in the living room and lay happily in the exquisite quiet. The moon had left its high spot and a mix of stars filled the night sky. Some formed a bright mantle while others seemed weary and less determined. The thought of Molina being only a room away sent Cameron's thoughts to her scent that lingered long after she had left a room. Would this be my last opportunity to speak to her and let her know of his love? But the travel and the whisky began to take its toll and he drifted into a pleasing dream of a narrow road he seemed to recognise that led to the edge of a shaded wood and to a quiet river. He was sure he knew where it was, his recognising the path filled with red leaves scattering in the breeze seemed to assure him. But the certainty began to fade along with the dream and he was once more curious of the place in the dreams. Cameron would have this dream many times over the next few years but got no further than the identical spot each dream. And yet he still felt a feeling of peace and security was it not strange he thought of being comforted in a place he may have never seen and yet?

After a breakfast of fresh ham and eggs Cameron was ready to visit his mother and father. Before he left Larry asked him about Geordie. Cameron told him, "He is following some trail of missing evacuee's. The report is of two boys and a younger sister. He will be working with the police in trying to unravel the last few minutes they were last seen. Geordie has a nose for that sort of thing; remember Sergeant Brown and the murder on the farm it was Geordie help bring all the pieces together to help in his conviction." He was sure that Geordie would be just fine as long as he didn't fall under the spell of a chorus girl. Cameron turned to have a look at the cottage as he walked towards the bus stop hoping to see Molina when he heard her car engine. She drove up to him and asked if he would care for a lift. Cameron sat taking in her sweet scented aroma of lily and watched her red coloured finger nails. He wanted to touch her arm but refused to allow himself in case she became angry and ended their friendship. Finally as the car approached his house he took his heart in his hands and told her. "Molina I must tell you this in case anything should happen to me. I love you and have done do since I saw you sitting in the grass." Before he could go any further she said "Thank you," as she braked the car suddenly and turned to face him. "Nothing personal Cameron, but we have been close for such a long time and it has remarkably taken you till now to tell me this. Then it can wait that much longer as there is a war on and you have things to do and I have a practice to run." "I'll drive you to the bus stop when you leave, till then have a nice time and give my regards to your Mum and Dad." She spun the car around and drove at breakneck speed towards the crossroads.

13.

Neighbourhood of Spies.

The days flew by seeing old friends and taking long walks with them in the hills. Ex-policeman sergeant Brown was notably on his list. The sergeant now lived in a bungalow not far from his parent's house. The sergeant's health had begun to wane but was keen to speak to Cameron. Cameron opened the conversation with a question on the murder he had published in the local rag. "Do you still believe one of the reasons for the murder of the foreigner was gambling?" The sergeant thought for some time before he answered. "I had information that there were German spies in Scotland at that time to find out information on the airfields and shipping ports, but how this would fit in with a murder and gambling I haven't the faintest idea." Cameron was slow to reply. "Perhaps we need more information to tie it all up?" The sergeant then added three of the men involved wore smart clothes and were seen talking to Molina and Robert the day before the murder. "Not that a hat or a conversation with people you meet every day means anything sinister." "Funny, neither Molina nor Robert ever mentioned this event, it must then have been something not worthy of telling or they had no wish to tell us the contents of the conversations. "Cameron was taken slightly aback by this news and did wonder why. "I think we should just leave it at that for the time being." Said a sleepy sergeant Brown sinking comfortably into the sofa. "There is just one more important point to make, my bonny lad." The sergeant said handing Cameron a report from Scotland Yard. The report explained Adolf Hitler's adjutant Fritz Wiedemann who had been sent to San Francisco after complaining about the Nazi plans for expansion had advised British Intelligence in America to strike hard at Hitler. By this he included the assassination of the German leader. He even offered to broadcast publically his denunciation of the Nazi schemes. But as America was not at war with Germany they were not interested. Britain mirrored this decision and lost a great opportunity. Cameron wanted more but knew he should not tax the old man. Spies, gambling and violent murder what was the connection? Other spies had landed in Scotland and were quickly captured. It seemed to carry ill fortuned from the beginning. At the end of their training the leader spy was killed in a drunken car crash. When two spies landed in a Heineken sea plane during bad weather they had to get rid of bicycles that were valuable to the plan throwing them overboard to avoid a sinking. At Portgordon Rail station they arrived with wet footwear and legs. They bought two single tickets and produced a wallet full of pound notes. The station master immediately called the local constable. But the whereabouts of a woman called Vera became mystery.

14.

Searching for myself.

Cameron enjoyed being at home with his parents and having a rest from the hectic city life. He didn't care about the weather which was always unpredictable at the best of times. It was exciting to have a quiet stroll before breakfast over the paths he had taken in childhood, stopping occasionally to drop in to see families that lived in the isolated moors. One of them was the Barkley family who lived in the semi abandoned Saw Mill. Jean was a widow of the Mill owner Stewart who had died ten years before. She and her daughter Moira refused to leave and taught themselves to use the mill sawing equipment. They scraped a living mostly by filling orders for the famers and making light weight durable wagons. They had four German shepherd dogs to guard the place that looked like a junk yard with twisted metal old cartwheels and ancient piles of damped timber. Cameron thought it unlikely that anyone would have dared to take on Jean notwithstanding the dogs. Jean was over six feet tall and slim often carrying an old shot gun. Moira was the mirror of her mother and could swing an axe as good as any man. He thought it was good that they were proud of their work and their ability to endure this desolate land. The women sat in wooden chairs chatting and enjoying the last of the year's sun. The dogs were in the garden and seemed asleep. Cameron asked the women if they felt safe. Both answered at the same time that they were happy and positive about living in the mill house. Given that assurance he then told them of the murder years back and the possibility of more than one murderer. "I hope this suspicion doesn't frighten you I felt its best you know anyway," Jean and Moira said sometimes in late evenings they would hear sounds from the fir trees if the wind was blowing from that direction. But the woodland was full of wild animals and flapping birds, more importantly no one has ever come near the mill after dark. "Not that I blame them with your dogs and the old shotgun." Cameron remarked to give them encouragement. Jean knew she could depend on her dogs said confidently "The dogs are natural at defending their property and would often explore any noise or movement especially at night so we have no qualms about being here alone in daylight or dark." After a strong coffee Moira indicated she had to go to bed soon as they had a busy day tomorrow. Cameron took the hint and shook their hands then bid them goodnight, naturally he invited them to his parents' house but reminded them they had better phone as they may be out on some interview. Jean asked them to be excused as they would be very busy in the near future. But they would gladly keep the invite in mind. Cameron had left his coat on a stand near a bedroom door and as he lifted his coat off he by chance noticed in the room a chair. On the chair was a Continental styled jacket. He managed to keep his composure and waved them goodbye at the gate. Darkness had come early and Moira seeing this insisted two of the dogs go with him to the top of the hill. He nodded approval and had to admit felt safe with the dogs running around him. Once he reached the hill top he could hear a faint whistle and the dogs stopped on their tracks then ran for all their worth back home. He had to admit he felt a certain sense of vulnerability after they had left.

The next day Cameron revisited Sergeant Brown. He told him of the jacket he had seen in the bed room and his plan to go back to the mill uninvited to see if there was more to the place than meets the eye. The sergeant considered Cameron's plan for some time before agreeing it may be helpful in uncovering clues. "But what of the dogs, won't they present some problem?" Cameron asked. "I'll invite them over, they like to come to see me and do some shopping while I look after the dogs. I don't see any great problem." Sergeant Brown was pleased he could help; he lifted his phone and began dialling immediately. "That's it fixed for tomorrow." With that certainty Cameron left to detail his own plans. In reality he wanted to find Jean and Moira above suspicion as he was quite fond of them and would miss his occasional drop in visits.

15.
Full of Incident.

The next day Cameron reluctantly made his way to the mill house which lay quiet in the midday winter sun. Getting into the house was easy as he had been trained for such an event. He searched the most logical places then more secretive hideaways. After a careful exploration he was relieved there was not a thing of criminal interest. Cameron thought it was possible he could even been wrong about the Continental cloths but there was a difference in war cloths in Britain easily identified and were now on the list to be rationed. It may have been a lover and idea of this brought a smile to his face. The front door opened and in came a youngish man. Both stood as if paralysed awaiting the other to move. In a startled voice the stranger said. "I'm a friend of Jeans and Robert." Cameron was trying to place the stranger as a friend of Roberts but without avail. "I've known Robert most of my life and I have never once met you, so you will have to try a different story." "My name is Peter and my country is Austria, Germany and Britain. I met Robert in Germany some years ago when he was involved in an incident." "What incident would that be?" asked an irritated Cameron?" "That I cannot tell, you must ask Robert" "Then why are you here in this house now?" Cameron knew he had to get to the bottom of this. Peter knew that the authorities would be after him soon so he willingly explained. "The man murdered years ago was a friend of mine sent to look after Robert, this I thought at the time a good idea. But we later found out he was a Nazi spy, and looking after Robert had a more sinister meaning. You see some people wanted Robert out of the way and did not want to wait for an amateur assassin to dirty work and so sent Max Hemmer a well-known servant of the Nazi party. But things went wrong and Max killed our friend the gambler who strangely looked so very like Robert. I for one thought it strange they should send someone like that, it is still a mystery. It may be a coincidence. This man we called the gambler and had years of experience in underground work, a man of this time when such skills are invaluable, so whoever killed him must have been good at his job." Peter lifted his head up and stared at the sky. "My father was a Scottish engineer in Germany where I was born and my mother an Austrian Jew from Salzburg who taught Mathematics, As a Jew she was at pains not to lose her job. Like Robert I did not know where my loyalties truly lied were they in the country I lived in and loved or the country of my parents." "Then you are a fool Robert is British to the core. That I'm certain of." While saying this Cameron he could not totally convince himself. There were too many rising doubts. One thing he was certain of is that he had to ask Robert of the incident he had so skilfully kept to himself. "You have avoided telling me why you are in this house right now?" Peter hesitated for a moment and then boldly spoke. "I'm in love with Moira and have been allowed to stay on certain days for which I am eternally grateful. Also I am frightened Max will return and you must know the Nazis' are not very charitable people." Cameron asked. "But why should they come to this house when all they have to do is wait for you to leave and ambush you." "Moira wrote to my father who is still in Germany and asked if I could help as she had noticed a change in Robert since his return and by doing so may have endangered her own life. It is easy to steam open an envelope as some of my father's employees have different political believes." "Let's get out of here and find a place where we can talk". Cameron realised the time was drawing near for the return of the girls and the dogs.

Once over the fields they were under the cover of the pine trees and were well hidden. Sound was muffled under the thick pines and pine carpet that covered the woodland floor. They sat on a log and smoked a cigarette before continuing their stories. "To begin with I must ask you not to run to the police until I complete my mission." Cameron had to agree with this as he did not wish to lose Moira or

Jean. "Remember to ask Robert to explain things as soon as you can, which is imperative as you will have only a hint of the story. Anyway if I should botch this mission I want you to finish it for me." Peter asked sincerely. "Are you British Secret Service?" Cameron was a little amused and answered he was a lowly newspaper reporter. But he wrung his hands in anguish at the thought of Molina and Robert in danger. He still felt that despite their conversations Peter was concealing vital information from him and Peter must realise the despair this episode was causing. "We must look for this man Max and stop him in his tracks. But I'm sorry to say as yet I have no real description of the Max. The only thing we can do is be on the lookout for strangers." Cameron wanted to relay his strong feeling to Peter and as if Peter knew this he sighed and added. "Maybe there is more than just the incident that Robert got involved in. He may be in greater trouble than we think especially when they want him dead." Cameron swallowed hard and vowed in his own heart to help Robert come what may. For the time Cameron had left of his leave from the London based newspaper he was willing to help Peter and also knew he had to be careful as the local inhabitants may be farmers but they were far from being fools. So while they both scoured the country side and villages for signs of a stranger they must not be suspected of anything intrusive. They also wanted to play safe and not cause an innocent person to be accused during war time. Word in the villages was of outsiders looking for work where labour was or about to be scarce. Not that it was unusual as after the harvest many freelance farm workers were sent packing. "I'm feeling good" said, Peter "And a bit peckish so if you know of some good eating house lets go." Cameron nodded in agreement and led the way.

The homemade soup of the Cottage Inn and fresh bread went down well especially when the innkeeper's wife gave them seconds. Peter thought it would be better to spend the night at the Inn so they could have a fresh start, to which Cameron happily agreed. In his dreams that night Cameron enjoyed an intimate talk with Molina while capturing Max and saving Robert at the same time all in one day. But the morning was cold and carried with it reality and a bitter wind. He knew that looking like holiday makers at this time of the year would not be easy. While Cameron made some hot tea, Peter dressed for the walk. Each busy in their own private thoughts. Cameron continued to think of some way he could help Robert but with the lack of information that was quite impossible. Peter knew how serious this problem was and had checked in the readiness of his revolver several times in secret.

They decided to walk to a farm in the south of the moor. But soon the new snowdrifts hampered their progress. The jokes about the prospect of having to spend a night in the open began to wear thin. "Sooner you than me," said, Cameron shouting above the wind which forced him to turn his head leeward. The skyline that only a few weeks previously presented a wild charm had now had changed to a bitter cold vengeful desert. The wind caught Peter mid breath causing him to wrap his hood over his face to allow him to catch his breathing rhythm. This blinded him for an instant causing him to slip on an ice covered rock, he fell brutally. His black revolver slid from its concealment over the white snow and stopped at Cameron's feet. Cameron had an unpleasant presentiment realising this was indeed a serious business and made him wish he had come armed. Peter picked up the revolver checked it once more and walked away silently. At the farmhouse near the end of the moor a man of short stature came out of the front door and walked to a large black sedan car. Cameron waved him over. The strangers face was red in the wind and his lips a light blue. As if to clear himself from any wrongdoing he told them in a thick Polish accent that he and his friend were over here for work. Then added they had all the correct papers to prove it. He sounded grateful to be in this country and appeared honest enough. Still he wished they kept quiet about their whereabouts in this present climate. The Pole's friend came out of the house. He was large and walked quickly to their car as speedily as he could as if it were urgent. The stranger told Peter and Cameron they should leave as they had business to attend to rushed to clutch the shoulder of his companion and swore under his breath. Both then returned to the farmhouse to uplift some items then proceeded to the sedan and drove off. Cameron knew it would be a waste of time waiting for their return so they drifted off towards the town. After a short while Peter mentioned about the big man swearing. "It sounded to me even in the wind as if he said 'neugierige schweine which is German for 'nosey pig.' "So much for them being Polish and all their papers being correct and I have to say I did not like the attitude of the big man at all." Cameron sounded angry. At this moment in time Cameron's instincts were to call on Sergeant Brown but he had told Peter he would not mention his name to the Police. As he was beginning to trust Peter he told him of his thoughts. Peter, in some ways agreed but pointed out he had a gun and on a mission to eliminate Max not for his own interest but to prevent anything undesirable happening to Robert. Cameron asked, "When will you have a description of Max?" Peter explained he was waiting for a reply from his last radio contact with his father in Germany, who would supply all the latest details about Max. At least we have two suspects more than we had yesterday." It was Sunday and the village church was spilling its good folk on to the road. Cameron and Peter melted in with the cheery chattering local girls enjoying the banter and the joys of youth especially the young girls dressed in their Sunday refinery. This was a feeling Cameron was beginning to appreciate more and more.

For Cameron the last of his leave was coming to an end and all he could think about was reporting the result of the meeting with the two men to Sergeant Brown, but his instincts held him back yet he was not totally convinced they were correct.

16.

A dependable Philosophy.

Before he knew it time had flown and it was time to go back to work in London. Molina picked him up and drove off slowly, the old car rattled as it encountered each bump or snow filled pot hole. Cameron could feel time slipping away and knew he had to say something; he turned to Molina almost surprised at her sweet face. "Have you anything to say on the subject of love? You see I have made up my mind to eventually persuade you to marry me. It would be the best thing in your life." Cameron was surprised how confident he sounded. "I will write to you each day and tell of my thoughts and hopes. Please Molina, do the same if you wish." Molina reminded Cameron there was a war on and no one knew how it may end up. Molina said after a space that seemed interminable, she would write. This was more than Cameron had expected and replied. "I agree there are no certainties in this nutty war, but I do know how I feel and that is the most important thing." Unlike their other departures he touched her hand and she responded by holding his fist against her cheek. His heart was now lifted to its highest level feeling self-assured and with a purpose in his life.

As the old car ran down the narrow road to the river crossing another vehicle approached from behind. It was a large black sedan. Molina was shocked at anyone would be foolish enough to try and over take on this slim road bracketed by high hedges. The sedan roared to parallel them. Cameron tried to make out who the driver may be. But it was impossible as the refection of the darkened bushes swept across the sedan windows. There was a limit to the road as it turned sharp right to the wooden bridge and then came a steep hill all this was now about five hundred yards away. The sedan scraped against the old car pushing it towards the bushes. Cameron heard himself saying quite calmly 'ram them, ram them.' As if practiced, Molina put her foot down on the accelerator and waited till the sedan came near again. Then with all her strength Molina turned the steering wheel sharply towards the sedan. The sudden impact caught its driver unprepared sending the black car hurtling thought the high hedge and down to the river. The river was in spate due to the melting of the midday snows and easily carried the sedan with it. A window of the sedan slid down and Cameron recognised the fat man as the man he had met on the train so well dressed and giving so sound advice. He was shocked and weirdly saddened at the look if hate on his face. He made an effort to open the car door as hugged the riverside but it was hopeless. The car crashed against a protruding old rotten tree sending branches and mud high in the air. The car overturned screeching and battering to slip into the deeper part of the river. Then all was quiet except the rush of waters and Molina crying. What to do and what could be done passed both their minds but knowing full well there was no positive answer. To go near the river at this time would be suicide. The river had that ancient spell of dangerous spirits larking just under the surface awaiting some fool to look too close. Its, clasping hypnotics were ready to take you down to the dark slow moving bed of mud. Where you will stay or return days later in a different form. Molina was the quickest to return to some sanity and prevailed on Cameron to look a bit further downstream for a sign of life. He did so reluctantly. Once out of the car he felt uncomfortable as if he the living had no right to be here in this dark place. The wind whipped branches of sodden leaves on to this face as he moved gingerly in the mud. It was as if the mud was in cahoots with the river to capitulate a naive walker into the wild waters. After a short time he realised the car and its contents were as gone as Babylon. He hurried as quickly as possible to the warmth of the car and the nearness of Molina. She was still sitting with her hands on the steering wheel and her head on her hands. "Look, Molina we can't sit here all night hoping things will change, I have to get to a phone to call my boss in London and arrange to see Sergeant Brown. As well as picking up Peter, you know him of course? We have to report this incident to the law and get it sorted out now, today." Molina agreed there was nothing else for it, and then she drove off not wanting not caring to look back once.

Sergeant Brown listened to the story of Peter and Cameron naively looking for Max the assassin and then the sedan and the river incident. He picked up his phone and called a local inspector. When the inspector arrived Brown took him into to another room. Peter and Cameron could hear the trio of voices but not enough to know what they were saying. They looked at each other feeling guilty of not having informed the police from the beginning. If they had done so the outcome may have been different, or so they thought. The sergeant and the inspector came out of the room with dark faces. The inspector was first to talk. "You now know the circumstances of your actions. I hope this is a lesson well learned and never to be repeated. The law is not a game, remember that. Sergeant Brown restated the substance of the advice they had been given also how disappointed he was in Cameron's council. He stood up and told them to leave and never to discuss what happened with anyone including their parents. Peter said what the others were thinking. "We were like bloody amateurs in a dangerous division." Cameron fastened to the philosophy of Sergeant Brown.

17.

True Adventure goes forth aimless.

Back at the Express in London the editor called both Cameron and Geordie into his office. "Gentlemen I have an assignment for you. As you know much is being debated about the nature of Maginot Line. You youngsters will have the uncommon pleasure of telling the national of its merits and if any it's possible down falls." Pausing a minute before carrying on as if to gather his thoughts and looking a bit concerned. "You see we have something to live down gentlemen. In August of this year we had the headline 'No War this Year.' Looking back I think we were given the wrong information by our Berlin Chief Correspondent Mr Panton. So we need to get it right this time. "Cameron nodded. "We will do our best and can we have a few days in Paris on the way back?" The editor smiled and agreed. "I would have been very disappointed in my Newsmen if you hadn't asked that, you never know what you can pick up on a fishing trip." Geordie was so excited he talked well into night until Cameron began to snore. He had told Cameron of the missing children during the evacuation.

The children were evacuees on the way to Northumberland but somehow got on the wrong train. Alarm bells had sounded and anyone looking the least suspicious was dragged in for questioning. A railway guard on a southern train had questioned the missing children and had them taken to a police station in Cornwall. The local people had made a big fuss of the children some baking buns and others supplied lots of fresh milk and foods. The local council asked if anyone would be interested in looking after the children until such times it would be safe for their return home. A Mrs Calvert on her way back home to Plymouth said she would be delighted to take charge of the children. After being questioned by the police and council she was allowed to take them with her. "We were glad that it ended happily with the two brothers and sister together and would be playing happily somewhere in Plymouth, far away for the capital." Geordie, found some comfort in the image of the children playing in a park, with Mrs Calvert looking responsibly and lovingly on.

In was early in the morning when Cameron heard the doorbell. Hurriedly he made his way downstairs in his pyjamas. He was astounded to see Robert and Molina. Molina walked past Cameron and hugged Geordie who was still part asleep but managed to say "Ah!" Then added, A beautiful woman calling at a uncivilised time of five thirty just when we were about to make breakfast, but an embrace quashes any complaints." He could barely make out the time on his wrist watch. "But what brings you here?" Geordie asked as he ushered them in towards a seat. "Our father thought this would be a great opportunity for you to show us around the city." Robert said smiling at the thought. "You have just timed it right as we will be leaving on an assignment in two days' time." "Is it exciting?" asked Molina." "Oh! Just the Maginot Line and its mysteries and some time in that wonderful city of Paris to recuperate, but I promise to look after young Cameron here." Geordie said this proudly before going to the fire and giving it a good poke to enliven it. Cameron couldn't help himself from asking. "There is more to this than the sites of London? If so let's hear it." Robert laughed. "I have to see and old friend just back from Berlin who happens to be a doctor and Molina wants an opinion on a patient's medical matter, nothing mysterious."

Cameron and Geordie were determined to give Molina and Robert a good time despite rationing which had begun in January. First on the odious rationing list were butter, bacon, ham and sugar then followed by meat and tea with restrictions on margarine and cooking- fat. Mostly, rationing worked well as the people of Britain took the austerity in their usual humorous spirit. Organisations sprung up to help in London, in particular the Women's Volunteer Service (WVS) who ran clothing exchanges, rest centres and very useful to strangers to the capital as an information bureaux's. Geordie asked a WVS girl the best places to eat and ended up with a date for himself and Robert. Cameron was very happy with this arrangement and hoped Molina felt the same. So far she had shown little interest in him and he wondered if there was something wrong. The food was passable and the London jokes about Adolf Hitler were as good as the plentiful comedy shows. One of the jokes was about Hitler visiting a lunatic asylum. As he passed each patient they gave the Nazi salute as he walked down the line of beds. But one person did not salute and Hitler shouted, "Why you are not saluting." The man answered, "I'm a nurse and I'm not crazy." Strangely, he heard this was one of the whispered jokes that came from Germany. There were a growing number of sandbags and trenches appearing in the most unlikely places, which could be dangerous in the dark. Overhead barrage balloons swayed in the winds and the people below in a changing London were increasingly carrying gas masks. These marked a war change in the capital. On the last night they were laughing at the latest rumour of the war as they strolled past Knightsbridge Barracks. Geordie said we could never beat the human ability to invent silly stories, such as the one about Hitler carrying a gun in his pocket to shoot himself if the war went wrong for him. Avoiding a mud heap Cameron inadvertently fell against Molina who smiled at him and pulled him closer. It was night full of stars that made him feel reflective and Cameron told Molina of his mood. Molina said she understood and put her hands behind his head and kissed him. "I can always say we kissed under the London stars." Cameron answered, "And I loved you for it." They strode hand in hand passed the Wardens and rows of singing soldiers, singing the old first war ditty 'It's a long Way to Tipperary.' Cameron wondered how long it would be before a new song would be sung about this new war. "I wouldn't have changed tonight for all the tea in China." Cameron whispered into the wonderful scented ear of Molina who looked so beautiful and touchingly happy. He took her hand and put them in his pockets as he stared at her wonderful green eyes spellbound.

But thoughts interrupted his spell. It was strange the effect of the Phony War has in our daily life, we naturally expected it to be different and it was but in an unlikely way. Where were the bombers that were expected the first fortnight of the war that would destroy the city in a night? It was a dreamlike quality when the sirens wailed the Alert in a warning and then the worry till the All clear is sounded. But they did not come. We all felt that the channel had prevented a lightening attack that had befallen Poland, yet we still had to guard the coasts obvious points and the air space above the channel. After the anti-climax came a feeling there was no war at all. Still changes were made, letterboxes where painted with pigments that would change colour if poisonous gas was detected. A call in every newspaper to carry your gas mask at all times was to some extent obediently obeyed and ARPs enthusiastically made sure we did. But some just carried in the gasmask shoulder bag their lunch or books to read on the train and who could blame them as there was no war. There was a tale of a small boy going in a pigsty to test his gas mask and we were sure there were many more crazy stunts not reported. Sometimes we felt irritated by petty rules and equally petty enforcers. The black out for no planes was one of those things we found to be a bit over the top and not only that it was bloody dangerous. Cameron and Molina arrived back at the flat and promptly put the light on before closing the curtains and pulling over a blackout. "Put that bloody light out," came from below and they jumped to put the blackout in place. Molina noticed that nearly all the blackout windows in the street closed tighter in response, it was a guilt thing they all shared. A policeman had arrived at next door and hammered on the door and when the door was finally opened the light spilling out nearly blinding the policemen, a few words were exchanged and then the lobby was an eyrie dark, followed by the thump of boots along the corridor. Cameron noticed his sense of sound had enhanced greatly and he could hear the footsteps of those approaching the flat some distance away. He could hear voices in the distance and recognised them. Geordie and Robert arrived just in time for the news on the radio. The same could be said from outside as the whole street had tuned into the same BBC station at the same time. Geordie remarked that it was difficult to find their way up the street as the sky was heavily overcast and the streetlights were out and the vehicles with fitted with dimmers. He had a torch with him when he slipped on a wet pavement surface and dropped it; both of them had searched around with outstretched hands in the moonlight reflecting puddles that covered most of the roadways. A policeman and a warded joined in the search but had to give up as the rain began to fall once again. "Come back tomorrow and have another go, advised the policeman as he wiped his wet knees. Next morning brought him little luck and Geordie had to order a new torch and more prized batteries. Geordie wore a white patch on the back and front of his coat but this had little success and he still had to jump out of the way of cars and bikes when the light began to fail.

It was remarked that Hitler was winning the war on the cheap as so many people were being killed by accidents each night. Then the authorities had the sense to relent due to the number of fatalities and allowed some faint street lighting. A squad of soldiers had been killed one night by a butcher's lorry as they marched back to camp and caused a huge uproar. It was like a breath of sanity to Londoners when some light lessened the danger on the busy streets. Cameron had wanted to get Molina a gift before their departure and had some discomfort looking into boarded shop windows with peepholes. Finally he decided on a pair of knitted gloves for the oncoming winter. He asked the help of an elderly lady the direction of a good woollen shop. She was kind enough to take him by the hand to find a local shop. She was more agile at climbing steps and walking in gloomy lanes than Cameron. He had to admire her ability and sense of direction in the dark maze of that part of London's Streets. He was now sure after the example of the elderly lady that the rest of London would to adapt to any changes the war might bring. The shop was run by an enthusiastic woman who was in the WVS. She told him that knitted gloves and balaclavas were becoming the vogue and were a sensible gift as there was now a make and mend culture and the gloves could be repaired. But what was especially true at nightfall and in the early morning a damp cold hung in the air.

Molina was delighted with her freshly knitted red gloves and had never expected Cameron to have thought of such a sensible gift. As a reward she placed a warm kiss on Cameron's cheek. "We will meet again and have some time together away from ARP's and shouting wardens. Somewhere we can talk in peace. I think we deserve at least that." Cameron shouted this to Molina in mad house of Kings Cross station as she found a seat in the crowded carriages. But he was unsure if she heard, as the noises were overwhelming. As she waved from the sooty window of the crowded carriage she grinned apologetically. When the train moved off the whole carriage waved at him all laughing at the solitary figure with the love lost expression. After leaving the station Cameron and Geordie prepared for their expedition to France. Then the evening was rounded off with an office party that surprised them when it lasted till dawn. They both staggered to the apartment for a few hours' sleep before the taxi arrives to take them on their way.

18.
A Glossy Surrealist War.

In France they discovered the thoughts of the people were opposite to the British. They had very little interest in invaded Czechoslovakia as the public's eye was still on the results of the Spanish Civil War. A huge influx of fit and wounded Spanish refugees tumbled into France. Some dying without the help they needed and others homeless were digging holes in the sandy beaches for shelter. France, Cameron discovered had stayed out of the Civil war to avoid one of her own, which may have been the right thing to do but as usual there were penalties to be paid even for doing nothing. But German and Continental activities in Spain had made many a Frenchman think especially when Marshal Petain had been sent as ambassador. Franco had just ignored the Marshal sending the ex-Mayor of Bilbao to meet him. This was a direct insult in retaliation to the Spanish fleet being interned by the French in Bizerte. All of this was happening next door to France and seemed more important to the ordinary people and the politicians than Czechoslovakia and other growing catastrophes. Driving to the Maginot line the correspondents took in the pleasure of the green rolling French country side. Even the weather made them welcome with a sun that was gentle and warm. Geordie and Cameron stopped at some of the farms to eat local foods and drink the local wines. They heard the country people talk of Daladier their Premier as a man to respect and one who would sort things out with his full personal and governmental powers. Geordie saw the similarity with Britain in the belief that a strong leader would surely soon solve the problems that were mounting up almost daily. They studied the plans of the Maginot line that duly unfolded its apparent strengths and inherent weaknesses. Both of the correspondents approached their study of the great defensive structure with seriousness as they knew of its eventual importance The Alsace-Lorraine part of the Maginot line had taken ten years to build during the 1930s. Later it stretched from Switzerland to Longuyon to where the Ardennes forest begins. The Ardennes forest was considered by the military experts of the time as impassable especially for armoured vehicles. There were also monetary considerations during this time that blunted the ardour of continued building. Anyway the forest was hilly and credited as having no significant value to an invading force that required armour, so what would be the point of spending good money on the project unnecessarily. It was certainly still impressive; there was no doubt about that. The formidable structure had led the Germans into building their own version called the Siegfried line and this obviously made it obvious to any doubters the Maginot Line was the future in defensive warfare. The German Siegfried Line was 390 miles long and had 18,000 pillboxes and tank traps 3,417 were 5 foot thick. In 1940 a reconstruction of some of the line made it one of the greatest defensive structures on this planet. One thing Cameron and Geordie agreed on was its massive difference compared to the first war old trench systems which exposed troops to rain and hindering mud. Within the Maginot line the troops lived in air-conditioned apartments complimented with a recreational area. More importantly all the compartments were connected by an underground rail system allowing speedy transportation. It had its water supply, hospital and to deter the enemy infantry traps and thousands of anti-tank metal domes. The Maginot Line had reminded Lord Alanbrooke of a battleship built on land. Geordie considered the description as eminently correct, the outward appearance was that of a great ship that would withstand and repel the enemy with ease. But when Cameron wrote of this gigantic structure he emphasised the false security it gave the French people. He considered the money dumped on the static ground rather than on a modern mobile armoured force and just as important since the German invasion of Poland more improved and modern aircraft. He did not feel elated at his report, more of a disappointment of the time and money wasted on an idea that was out of date since Verdun. He hoped the newspaper editor would see his point of view but he knew that news of this kind would cause some panic especially to the general public hungry for confidence even if were a blatant lie. But news is news and he would wire it to London from the City of Light and grandeur, Paris.

When Cameron and Geordie reached Paris it seemed dull compared to their expectations as if it had lost much of the vibrancy and life. It was always written about in books and magazines as the place you must visit and as a famous author wrote, where all good Americans go when they die. People, Geordie noticed moving about the city famous throughout the world for its romance and charm were now well aware of the dangers of war. They were quickly becoming withdrawn. Geordie was the first to notice even the famous clubs were anything goes were subdued. Talk in the usually noisy Cafe's was of the young men that had been called up since Czechoslovakia. More worrying was their attitude to Hitler. "He won't bother us if we keep out of trouble." "You'll see it will all blow over soon if we keep out of Her Hitler's way." The women were also quick to repeat the old adage. "If women had been in charge there would be no wars." One elderly man stood up and took off his cap and said, "Women are involved you surely have heard of the cabinet of mistresses." To Cameron's dismay appeasement that had haunted Britain was still alive and well. To add to the misunderstanding of the events it appeared the French thought the British were militarily inferior to them. As if the last war had been won by the French alone and they were quick to add that Britain was an over exaggerated power. "We French know how to fight and like the last war we will destroy the bosh." A common cry was 'The English will fight to the last Frenchman.' The Germans were quick to take this up and use it as propaganda hoping to widen the gap between the allies and promote uncertainty. The women of Paris would gather and look to the white posters pinned to wooden posts to see if their men were on the new call up lists. Should he be on that list he had to leave for duty that day leaving the livelihood of the family to the care of the women wither they were country folk or city dwellers. Just as in Britain the rail and bus stations were crowded with soldiers who truly believed they were the best trained in the world and were therefore ready to face the enemy right now. But to married men there was that additional and lingering worry of how their families would now survive. They knew the wives would have all the added responsibilities of coping with the house and its upkeep as well as feeding their children on a meagre soldiers pay. Wives were astounded at the speed their husbands and sons left and had met in numbers on street corners to console each other and to look around to the streets near empty of males. Nearly half of the Paris population had left by car, bicycle or foot. Some said a famous Parisian lady resolved to write poetry and others contemplate suicide such was the imagined unreality of the insanity of a distant threat hanging over their everyday life. Woman all shared the uncertainty of their husband or sons return in this new world of war. Robert and Geordie spent some of the time trying out French wine, on one occasion Cameron found Geordie sitting in a toilet reading a French newspaper upside down. To sober up and get their wits back they walked through Paris and by chance saw a mass of foreign soldiers. Her colonies had sent their soldiers who would face German guns once again.

With the collapse of Poland some 120.000 troops and their air force escaped through the Rumanian Bridgehead Operation and were evacuated to France. Along with them were some of the Enigma code breakers that would have a serious effect on the Germans intelligence capabilities. To a newspaperman this was a great opportunity to ask about the German war machine and both the correspondence took full advantage of the situation. It was now well known the British would soon face the German war machine that had refined its attacking method to the extent it had not been stopped. Britain had signed a treaty to protect Poland and now it was time to be as good as its word. The Germans knew Britain would not walk away from its responsibilities; a country with a vast history of defiance and despite the greater odds against it would fight to the end. One of the escaped polish officers was glad to find someone interested in their plight in the maze of the Paris. Aldona Zajac was an aristocratic figure full of dash and confidence who had suffered the great humiliation of defeat by a bunch of what he called inferior deceivers. Aldona told them that rumours were abounded in Poland that the Germans had intentions of evading. Also that Poland in response was in an increasingly angry mood to the continued invisible German threats. Ribbentrop, Nazi Foreign Minister had hinted to the Russians on an understanding to the fate of Poland. This reassured the Russians as they would share some of the conquests treasures. With this in mind Hitler ordered a provocative note to be sent from Danzig to Poland on a dispute about customs officers. The Polish reaction was just as Hitler hoped for. Soon he received a warning that should anything happen to their customs officials in Danzig this would be treated as an act of violence against the Polish State. Later the German Ambassador to Berlin sent a note from the German authorities protesting on the interference by Poland on Danzig affairs. The Polish government were in no mood to be bullied and told the Germans if they dared intervene in the dispute it would be seen as an act of aggression. Aldona braced his shoulders back to look taller than he was in natural pose reminding Cameron that the Polish army was convinced they could defeat the Germans at their own game. With instructions from Hitler Danzig provoked a break with Poland at 04.30 on august the 26th set as zero-hour for his attack. But Hitler heard of the British –Polish alliance and at the same time of Mussolini's demand on more supplies. Hitler was furious and cancelled the attack date. The Fuhrer had one more trick up his sleeve and that was to draw the Poles into a negotiation and break it off blaming them. Added to this plan and a Swiss Birger Dahlerus would relay this blame to Britain that Germany would now have every excuse to break her promise with Poland and to leave the threatened country isolated.

19.

Poland is dead.

The real attack began at 04.45 on the 1st September. Aldona explained the Germans had developed the Blitzkrieg, a lightening war of speed and shock. That not only amazed the Poles but the Germans themselves. "The basis was to cut off supplies. The infantry attacked while laying down a smoke screen which was mostly to conceal the mass attacking armour. Dive bombers and paratroops cut off the reserves. Assault troops and demolitions destroyed the strong points allowing the armour to move through them. Motorised infantry and artillery would then play hell with the defenders while Dive bombers cleared the area in front of the tanks destroying the reserves and communications. Then the armour would fan out to destroy the enemy rear and key points cutting off command units, supplies and reserves, all controlled by wireless communication by excellent Generals. The German army had 11 armoured divisions 40 infantry divisions 4 motorised divisions 850 dive bombers and ordinary bombers with 400 fighters. All Poland could muster up front was 400 aircraft, all but round 36 were completely obsolete. As for light tanks 225 modern and 88 obsolete. 534 reconnaissance carriers and 100 armoured cars all obsolete. Many of our machine guns were outmoded, certainly our artillery was new but off poor quality and range. Communications were done through civilian telegraph and phone lines. We did not at first want to give the Germans an excuse to attack so arranged for three quarters of our forces to be called up with 72 hours' notice. Remembering about a third of our forces were cavalry units. So you can see gentlemen we did well to resist for so long." "Indeed." A sympathetic Cameron agreed while thinking of the events that had taken place over such a short time. "But we heard from other sources the German troops especially the officers were not keen on the war but Hitler overrode their hesitations. Hitler believed in his intuition and forced them to agree on Operation White the plan to attack Poland, a country the British had given assurances to. The attack had to be swift and superior. A bold and daring army with armour superiority never seen before coordinated from beginning to end. Aldona knew that Polish Chief Marshal Rydz-Smigly's plan would be defensive so that he would have time to gather his army's strength to counter attack. When the Marshal was told of Polish defeats and units cut off he replied to one of his generals. "General, it's too bad nothing can be undone, but we must hold out." But the advance had been so swift and effective it was difficult to counter. On the 17th September the Russians moved into Poland surprising the Germans and Poles alike. At first the Russians appeared much less aggressive than expected giving the rumour they had come to help the Poles and to take on the Germans. This of course was not so and the plans for retreat was then given."

20.

For every Good Reason there is a Lie.

Cameron and Geordie strolled down the Avenue des Champs-Elysees towards the Seine taking in the evening atmosphere. They talked about home and how the year had changed their lives so much. Geordie remembered the Dutch War Scare at the beginning of 1939 when an Admiral leaked information that the Germans intended invading Netherlands so that they could use Dutch air-fields to bomb Britain. "It caused a bit of fuss and the government sat up to take notice." "Mussolini decided to conquer Albania in April while we carried on living as if the world had not changed a bit. We still had village dances and gala days not to forget sitting in the sun eating ice-cream while the children sang and played." In their room they typed the day's reports as the sun went down and the lights of Paris flicked on. The phone rang. Reluctantly Cameron rose from his chair and listened. "It's Robert, I'm in trouble it's something to do with my visit to Germany some years ago that's all I can say at the moment." "Robert, have you contacted Molina? Cameron asked. "Not yet because she might tell the family and that is the last thing I want." Robert was clearly worried and needed a friend. "Well, call her as soon as you finish this call she should not be left in the dark." Cameron demanded. "We are due back in London next week so call Molina and stay at our apartment till we arrive, you should be safe there." "Thanks I'll do just that," with those final words Robert clicked off. "I wonder what the trouble is and did not want to say over the phone?" Geordie took his eyes off the type writer and replied. "We will know soon enough, it never rains but pours."

Back in London Robert had phoned Molina and asked her to come to London to see him. Instinctively she sensed there was some kind of problem and told her parent that Robert had a flu and she wanted to help him, after all she was his doctor. "Make sure he is on his feet before you leave and is eating well." Her dad asked. "I will and I hope to see the newsboys when they return from Paris. They will be as good as a tonic to Robert." Her dad drove her to the rail station and waved her off. He was not convinced and was concerned about the way she had lied about the flu. It was something in her hesitancy between her words especially the word flu. He knew her to be honest and would only lie to help someone and that someone must be Robert. Being a doctor he was used to keeping secrets but this one was a worry and was more than personal.

The train journey was not as exciting as previous trips. This time Molina felt weary and cold as the door windows and carriage windows were carelessly left opened by passengers in a hurry and less mindful of others. The cold fresh air rushed into steamy full to capacity coaches making the occupants shiver. The train was pulled by some ancient engine that had problems with its heating abilities. It crawled through the night stopping every now and again in a wilderness of black. Outside was countryside so desolate it might have been Siberia. It was smoky and noisy with occasional noisy bursts of conversation and in the distance Molina could hear the reframe of a sentimental popular song. Some soldiers tried to sleep off their apparent hangovers; their heads nodding against the head rests before settling on the shoulder of the adjacent fellow passenger. While others played noisy cards games to pass the time exchanging insults at the loss of a hand. She felt much better when she reached London where the people looked real compared to the train occupants. It felt like a new world compared to the ghostly buffeting fridge like train carriage. When she left the taxi and made her way to find the apartment in the dark her heart began to pound. A feeling of apprehension began to sweep over her; it was a feeling that sapped her body energy. But this feeling miraculously evaporated the instant Robert answered the door. Nothing could have stopped her from giving him a warm hug. A light meal was just what she needed and soon they began to talk. "Please let me know why you sent for me so urgently Robert." Asked Molina who was clearly concerned and hated each minute he made small talk that only exacerbated her patience. Finally Robert got down to brass tacks. "Have you heard of Walter Buch an important henchman of Hitler? Martin Bormann married Buch's sister Gerda. Hitler was one of the witnesses to the marriage. Buch was the one who made murder of anyone they took a dislike to appear legal in the eyes of the new Germany. He was naturally well rewarded by the Fuhrer who liked to follow the law when it suited him. He was also responsible for the parties work during Kristallnacht (Crystal Night). He has the knack of making things appear legitimate so affectively he made the murder of 100 Jews seem like an act of patriotic duty. According to Walter Buch those Jews were not human and were not suited to the new Germany.

21.

Some days are lost.

"What has that got to do with you?" Molina asked in dismay. Robert settled into his seat and looked her in the eye. "You see I was there on Kristallnacht on the 9ᵗʰ September in 38 with three of my German friends, two were officers in the SS and the other Buch. At that time I was a Nazi party member and so were nearly all my friends." "How is that possible?" Molina asked shaking her head in disbelief. "I have some German blood in my veins just as you have and you knew as well as everybody else I visited relations and friends several times a year, I had nothing to hide. Any idea of war with Britain at that time was considered farfetched even stupid. On this occasion twenty of us were very drunk and we got carried away with the destruction of a Jewish shop smashing the windows and throwing the well-made statuettes on to the road, when an old man ran out waving a walking stick. To protect one of my friends I hit him and kicked him when he fell near a shop doorway." I was astounded how little it takes to render a person helpless. He laid on the ground like a rag doll his limbs twisted and his face looking up at me. I staggered back. He looked for the entire world dead. I had killed a Jew for no reason and now had become one of the Nazi disciples. It was then that I discovered that another person was in the shop doorway. Imagine my surprise when I discovered he was Mohammad our mothers long lost lover, the one supposedly lost in the South American jungles. Even under the torchlight's it was possible to make out his fine Egyptian features and that look of authority or self-satisfaction men with piles of money seemed to have. I dragged him from the entrance of the shop and saw the objects we had thrown around were Egyptian statuettes.

Some I could see were of a female bust with a large head piece. Two bulky SS men pulled me away and true to form the SS companions congratulated me for the destruction of a Jewish pig. That was the words they used but I was unsure if I had killed him. The next day I took walk to the shop to see the damage not only to the property but this ex-lover of my mothers. I had no feeling for or against him before but now with the physical violence that made me hope he was still on the planet. He was sitting on an old chair that creaked as he rocked in and out of the sunbeams that danced in a vital light piercing into the darkened shop. Robert could see he had been damaged as his hands and arms black and blue shook involuntary. "This what becomes of you if you stray an inch out of line with the Nazi Party." I have been a member of the Egyptian Radical Nationalists since nineteen thirty four and a good friend of Husayn our leader. We were the green shirts and established on the same lines as the Nazi Party. Germany in time became my enemies' enemy growing more anti British with each passing year. When the organisation was disbanded in nineteen thirty eight some of us went underground and continued our connection to the Nazis Party. When we discovered Hitler's love of Nefertiti we immediately set up this shop in Berlin. "But there is more to this involvement with the devil my good friend." We thought we could steal the march in taking the finds after they had done all the work as we Egyptians often do.

Hitler despite his natural instinct's which had been mostly correct at the beginning of the war and told in Nazi tales as completely true. It was an enduringly wonderful epic in detail. He was in a true sense a believer in mystical objects and prophecies. In his Spartan room he would contemplate the fate of the world. If only he could lay a hand on a sacred object with the ability to make his dreams come true. Thus the mighty Hitler of the thousand years Reich was emotionally attracted to the ancient Egyptian queen Nefertiti Hedjet. In his dream of a New Berlin designed by himself and Albert Speer, who was his first architect and with his help would build a World Capital Germania after the war. Some years before Hitler sat in Berlin's Egyptology part of the Museum and inspired by the features and beauty of Nefertiti he had thought of the new great city. It was displayed in the Berlin Museum where he sat one day and had a photograph taken. Later he informed Eberhard von Stoher he was an admirer of Nefertiti and to let the Egyptians know of his admiration for the masterpiece, a true treasure. He considered the bust as a proof that Egypt was the genesis of Western Civilization. Hitler intended to build new museum in Berlin with a large dome with Nefertiti as centre palace. In his own words he stated, "I will never relinquish the head of the queen."

In Leipzig the German Egyptologist Walther Wolf who had pro-Nazi interests saw this was the way to get on in the new world Nazi German culture. He was not above lecturing in his SA uniform to show the length of time he was a supporter of the party. Like his kind, he was not interested in the pure Egyptologist study, more important was the link he expected to find to radicalize with the Volkagemeinshaft. He was sure what shaped the Egyptian culture was owed to the principle of blood and soil (Boden und Blut) similar to the Nazi Brotherhood of Blood. Nazis hopes were to find a force lying dormant in the national collective of its people waiting to be set free. In fact this was the same idealism used by the Pharaohs themselves. The actual work was not done by the Germans but the Egyptians themselves. While others like Hermann Junker went on digging sprees. Junker was almost free from German restrain and made the plans for investigating purely for and by him. Junker knew that the German government used the digging sites to contact various Arab movements to their advantage. To spread their bets the Nazis had appeared in other parts of the world with the same Blood ideology to find the Nazi link with them. Then they would have more than just an ally, they would be of the brotherhood.

In a far off digging some eleven miles for the Valley of the Kings some locals had managed to reach a thing of interest only ten feet down. In the midst of dust and small pieces of sandy rock they spotted a skeletal hand with wrapping of worn cloths. Inside the cloth were a blood mark and a clump of clay. There were three pharaohs each one after an exacting examination had died of some kind of affliction.

As if each one had been struck one after another and the misery had heightened to another level. Harlter a wild card Egyptologist was considered the one most likely to find the Aryan Blood factor and would win the attention of Hitler. As far as he could tell the diseases may have been caused by some insect bites on the thumb. The three pharaohs had a green crushed small insect remains near the left thumb and a blur on the remains of the skin that might have been an insect bite. But he could not be sure. After a thorough examination he came to the conclusion the Pharaohs had been murdered to prevent the spread of the disease they had died with. The bodies were taken back to Cairo and examined with a new thoroughness. In the end it was considered the Pharaohs might have been murdered intentionally and there was a possibility the microorganisms were still malignant. Yet, there was an underlying possibility of finding some latent power in use of the bacteria that the Nazis craved, and would use it without hesitation on the rest of the world.

Mohammad seemed very proud of his abilities as a thief when he added, it was during a lull in the German studies that we stole the bodies and left a note saying, 'We now truly departed.' And added, 'We are in a hurry to return to whence we came.' The bodies were transported to the other end of Egypt were the population is spars and the only ramblers are the shepherds attending small flocks of worn out sheep. It was so isolate it could have been back in the days before the great cities and the Nile still a mystery.

22.

Smokey Rumours.

An unknown Arab paleontologist wrote in a diary found on the windblown sand. 'Twenty days into our inquisitive study which was very amateurish compared to the Germans that things happened. Things we had never in a million years could have conjectured. Most of the desert tribes are very faithful to Allah, the one God, and do not allow the demon drink to touch their lips. While we Arab world travelers pretend to be faithful and partake in a little tipple drink. The truth is the party leaders of all kinds were all under the spell of the strong wine and as you say as, happy as Larry. We sat in comfort and enjoying the passing of a busy day. When out of the night a wild cry of distress was heard from the direction of the three now long dead Pharaohs. You do not have to be a genius to recognize wickedness at its height and we ran to see what had transpired. One of the dead Pharaoh's had been tilted I suspect by a wild inquisitive dog and appeared to be about to say something. His expression was of a determination to warn those involved in this circus in a narrow toothy grin. He did not point a finger since most of the hand was long gone. But I for one could see that the time to leave this unfortunate deed had come. Since then and from that exact second I then have never felt so alone, so very alone. Forgive me Allah for all I have been in my false pride, my foolhardiness has wasted the precious life you gave me. I then offered my life to Allah in return to be myself again and pray most earnestly, but even that does not seem enough. An Egyptian next to me slipped to his knees and whimpered, but I knew there was nothing under desert stars that would help him. A wisp of wind blew and the upright Pharaoh slipped to the ground and intermingled with the sand so that all that was left was ragged pieces of dirty cloth. The remaining body was hurriedly sent back to the Germans in Cairo with a covering note, 'Here you have what was taken by theft and retuned in dread.'

Little was heard of the studies made by Harlter and his Nazi fools until two months ago when the rumour's started to flow in the great hotels. At first there were whispered behind the back of a hand. Then boastful certainties of a discovery that will for sure change to course of the war.

Robert thought it was all hearsay with no real evidence. Smokey rumours were the bread and butter of the Middle East Cities the more ridiculous the better. Then being skeptical he blamed the whole episode on the Middle East temperament. He then blamed the romours on the inevitable war time conspiracies. Robert told himself it was time to put this kind of gossip behind and concentrate on his doctor studies. He never saw Mohammad again as he vanished into the dark of Berlin. He returned to his Nazi friends who still regarded him as a hero for killing a Jew, he didn't have the courage to tell them otherwise and let his reputation grow.

23.

Resign Yourself to Unsatisfied.

Robert added, "Just before the war broke out I wrote a letter to the Nazi party resigning from the moment from the moment the letter arrived at their headquarters. It never did end up in Germany and lay up in the old Post Office down at the end of the village near your house Molina. Later it was spotted by a Postal lad with the German address on it. He rightly took it to the police station. The police did not want to handle it considering it too hot to handle and had it delivered to the hush hush boys. I knew I was being followed and did not like the idea so London seemed the ideal place to hide. You may have heard it is now the ideal place for deserters to disappear in; there are now several thousand who have dodged the column. I asked for you to come so I could explain the situation to you personally Molina." Molina took her eyes of Robert for a moment before she answered him. "What did you put in the letter?" Robert sank to a seat his hands over his face. "I told them I was innocent of the murder of the Jew. Much later I found out a Jew had died in the same area and he had political connections in Britain, his father was of a famous London Jewellery dealer and had contacts with MPs." "How is that Molina? A murderer of a British man with a large rich and politically powerful family, what more can I ask for? To make matters worse I was sent a letter of congratulations from one of the top Nazis Walter Buch for topping a Jewish gentleman as he put it, trying to copy an English style. I'm sure the letter had been tampered with some months after I had returned. We corresponded for a while until Buch became entangled in more Nazi incidents." Robert looked abjectly sad and worried. "Do you know that now the war is here it may make

72

things difficult for those of us who have foreign blood? But it is not so for some in Germany, I met Baldur Von Schirach in Germany ten months ago who has an American mother and I'm told two of his ancestors signed the Declaration of Independence. His job is to turn the German youth into the Hitler youth so nothing is clear cut at all." Molina was not convinced he had been just a bystander in German politics. But, she would certainly help as he had been a good to her and their father, always ready to help. It's strange, she thought, he was always as open as a book but as they had now grown up he appeared entirely complex. Robert asked about Geordie. Molina smiled as if relieved he had changed the subject. "He is inspecting our coastal defences to keep us safe. I think there is only a few Torpedo boats so he won't be that long, were about as ready as a fish in a barrel."

When Cameron was told of the state of affairs Robert had got himself into he truly wanted to hit him. Not only for his blatant stupidity, which was serious enough but for letting down his sister and friends in a moment that could have been easily avoided. Larry, Geordie, Molina and Cameron listened to Roberts's explanation hoping to find a loophole or an excuse but there was none. "Let's all go out for a dinner." Molina asked. "Yes it may clear our heads and I think better on a full stomach." Larry answered. The Mount View Cafe in Lyons Corner House was very popular with its lighted pillars and wide spaces between tables. A waitress came from behind a pillar "What will it be?" "I'd like chicken with inions and boiled potatoes. Washed down with cool Pale Ale locally brewed and matured in oak barrels. Sounds very good but you'll have to go to the Chicken-Fayre for that love. You see that sign it says Cafe." Cameron knew of the reputation of the waitresses they were known as the Nippy's due to their impatience and downright cheek. Roberts said, "Let's go to the Flamenco Room the dinner show starts at 20.30 so if we hurry we will find a suitable table." The waitress shrugged her shoulders and shouted, "Fine by me, come again sometime never." Then she strolled off to another table totally unaffected in any way by the dissatisfaction of the customers, yet exceptionally pleased with herself at her offhand relies.

As the evening drifted on while the prettiest girls in London did their Spanish dances it occurred to Molina that Robert had indeed spent a great deal of time in Germany. This had been a time during the transition from a confused democracy to a fascist state. She remembered him telling her of the day they burned books at a University he attended in 1933. He told her enthusiastically German students associations loved to march down streets with lighted torches, as living stream of threats. This time they had declared against 'un-German spirit' and persisted it was now time to cleanse the Jewish literary world by fire. Prominent Nazis and professors in well planned speeches attacked Jewish intellectualism spreading the hatred far and wide from campus to campus and had been aided by free continual radio broadcasts. The plan was to accuse the Jews of smearing Germany worldwide and insulting her old traditions.

24.
Wars dirty little Secrets.

On the 10th of May 1933 some 25,000 books were burned as Un-German. Students and spectators threw the books on to the fires to joyous cheers while bands played, fire oaths vowed and songs sung. Robert had apparently enjoyed this episode singing heartily in the waves of torchlight and bonfire illumination. While the artists, musicians and Poets were being ostracised he had embraced the mobs values, caught up in the swiftly changing world. There was something special and moving in the new German culture that made him want to be part of it. Here he was in its midst grabbing a book and throwing it into the flames while his fellow students applauded. But for an instant the laminations lit up the Catholic Church nearby sending his conscious in a spin. He understood dark forces were playing near the sanctity of the church he had believed in all his life. Stranger still the church seemed neutral and unalterable at the same instant, this fleeting instance did little to make Robert come to his senses. He could only explain so much to Molina and missed out some of the real dilemma he was under. Molina was beginning to feel uncertain of Robert, even with her German relations being the same as Robert. She was still stunned by the murder of the man and was resolved to find some way to help restore Roberts's reputation and moral standing.

Thomas, Roberts's father arrived the next day and told Robert he must pack his things and come with him. There seemed no time for formalities or parental affection. This was clearly not a request, more an order that made Robert hurry to obey. Thomas Mason had been an amateur radio enthusiast at the outbreak of the First World

War and had an aptitude for picking up German Army and Navy signals. Code breaking at the beginning of the war was practically non-existent as there was no dedicated department in that field. The Director of Naval Intelligence Captain Henry Oliver was given the go ahead of setting up a department and finding someone to head the unit. He would look no further than his old Scots friend James Ewing a famous teacher, inventor and cryptographer. Ewing was keen to establish the departmental unit which was placed in the Admiralty room 40. The unit entailed a mix of eccentrics such as fellow Scots Alistair Denniston a famous German linguist, Thomas Mason and Irish novelist Hebert Morrah.

At the beginning of this second war a German battle cruiser had gone aground in the Baltic and some Russian sailors boarding her found German code books, which were sent to Winston Churchill then First Lord of the Admiralty. Soon the men in room 40 were off to a flying start reading the enemy signals and decoding with great success. But in a culture of professional jealousy in the naval department and MII (b) the Army equivalent, led to unforgivable inefficiencies. Most of this was the veil of secrecy both departments had created especially the unwillingness to share their finds. Reggie Hall was given the task of taking over from Captain Oliver. Hall had the habit of blinking and was known as Blinker.

It was during World War 1 and the German resumption of unconditional submarine warfare and after the sinking of RMS Lusitania that prompted German Foreign Secretary Arthur Zimmerman to cable the German Embassy in Washington so as to authorise him to negotiate a military alliance with Mexico against America. The message was picked up by room 40 and promptly deciphered. American President Woodrow Wilson on receiving the decoded telegram remarked, "Good Lord!" he knew that this meant certain war with Germany. But the part played by the Room 40 code breakers was more or less dismissed as many Americans at the time thought it just another British ploy to get them into the war. Reggie was most affected and out of the blue was reported to have remarked on the decoding of the Zimmerman telegram, "I alone did this." It was clear Reggie had the help of the code beakers to decipher the telegram and was far from alone. This observation of the goings on in Room 40 reached the ears of Thomas who had assumed they had always worked in compatible teams, felt betrayed and dismayed.

Thomas decided not long after the 'I alone' incident to leave Room 40 and reported to the British Secret Service. The Secret Service sent him on merchant ships as an agent-radio operator that sailed near to enemy coastlines. It was dangerous work but necessary especially with the advances in submarine warfare. When the war ended the naval and army departments were merged, Thomas stayed on as his old friend Alistair Denniston was now the new boss. Thomas assisted in the monitoring and decrypting of Russian submarine signals as his last assignment.

Now Thomas felt that it was time to return to his training as a doctor in Edinburgh, it was long overdue. In early 1920 he made his way home. He had made good friends and would miss them, just as he would miss the adventures and dangers in war. But he could not deny his first love had been medicine. Within a short space of time he threw himself into his studies, soon making a name for himself of being competent and reliable. At certain times he would communicate with his old friends in the now newly formed Government Code & Cypher School known as G C & CS. He felt that the comrades he had served with in war were irreplaceable. When he could find the time off he would pay them a visit in London.

When Thomas first heard of Roberts's ordeal he contacted some old friends and pleaded for them they work out a plan to save Robert. At first they had understandable reservations but he had insisted. Robert, he was certain might be of more use to the country because of his knowledge of the German people. Better that than being confined in a jail cell till the end of hostilities. He took no chances and escorted Robert to be interrogated personally, as he knew Robert might be tempted to vanish again into the masses of London. The interrogation was done by three men in dark suits for five hours mainly on his actions in Germany and his beliefs of Nazi superiority. The room seemed to get smaller as the minutes passed and his throat dryer. He knew he was in Baker Street and that was all. When it finally came to an end they insisted he should be sent for training immediately and that he should talk to no one of this interview as they called it. Robert called it an ordeal and was confused but glad he had not been sent somewhere to be punished or interned. He was going to be trained but as what and what would be expected of him?

Somewhere in the New Forest at a place called Beaulieu he was once again interrogated but in a more thorough manner. This time it was one of those Baker Street gents in an army suit. "You realise that prison is where you belong but we are in need of people who speak perfect German and know the culture. We especially require those who know their way around in that country and can travel on bus or rail without being seen to be an alien. This war has turned everything on its head. I knew your father and it's because of him and your talents I will give you this one chance. Fail it and you'll be lounging behind bars with your German friends. But in truth it may be much safer there."

25.
Strange choices.

He picked out each important detail of Roberts training as a doctor and as a traveller with local knowledge and excellent German skills. He particularly interested in his contacts and relations in Germany and admitted this was the swaying point as they have few good agents in the heart of the Reich.

Robert was trained with one other person, a woman of considerable beauty. That was one of the first things he noticed about the women agents they were well chosen for their looks and intelligence. Her name was Anna or so she said, and was a typist for an insurance firm in the midlands. Anna could speech German, Italian and French but was tight lipped about other details of her life. Just before their training began they were summoned to the man in the army suit. He explained they would be trained not only as spies but saboteurs. Primarily they were to gather information and send it to London as speedily as they could. Training to help the underground in explosives, observation and small arms would be part of their remit. Should it come to it they themselves would be expected to take part in the destruction of enemy property. Robert and Anna were sent from one training place to another to achieve the skills to do the job and hopefully survive. This last part seemed be less important than success of a mission. Recognising your enemy by their uniform and units by their shoulder flashes was useful to give the military intelligence of the enemy's whereabouts. Some of it was exciting for both of them such as safe breaking and how to break into a building without being seen or having the nerve to bluff your way through the front door if need be. Of course, elementary survival in the country by living off the land and how to build hides. Spotting a potential agent, that came under a different category as special skills of human observation and analysing were required. This was a skill where they learned there was no space for error of any kind. Should you be so unfortunate to make a mistake not only the spy but hundreds and maybe thousands could suffer. Other skills just as important were resilience, courage and resourcefulness as definite requirements. These had to be carefully honed before being dispatch to enemy territory.

Some of the instructors Robert was sure were assassins, and or hardened criminals. To be honest he hoped so, as he now understood this was total war and who cared for previous sensibilities. Woolly was the name of the main tutor, a person so well respected he was idolised. His brief was the teaching of amateurs on how to shadow, counter shadowing surveillance and how to pass messages without being noticed. It seemed as if hundreds of vital information had to be digested and fully understood or they were in real trouble. Robert and Anna played games in the streets, pubs and railway stations shadowing each other knowing a mistake soon may cost their young life. Anna being very pretty girl and known as a honey trap was allowed to move through the different departments freely and try getting information out of tutors and trainees then reporting her findings to Woolly. Being caught in the honey trap was goodbye to the unfortunate which served as a warning to them and just how easy it was to fall to the charms of Anna and her like. Anna never applied her wiles to Robert which he had hoped she would. He like many of the others was completely enchanted with her. He knew he was coming to the end of training when they were advised on the Killing Pill that was to be taken to avoid breaking up under torture, which thankfully took only a minute to take effect. Then they were instructed in how to behave in the enemy territory under differing circumstances especially if suspected. In case this did not work they were told how to use anything as a weapon including battery acid and to shoot to kill at short range. Practicing to sharp shot and how a knife should be aimed at the vital organs of the body followed.

Apparently the most dangerous job of all was the wireless operator who exposed his position the second they switch on the machine. They had just a fifty percent chance of returning. The skill of quickly tuning to a precise radio coordinate, relaying a message and then hiding the radio set made Robert hands shake in a cold fear. Learning how to fight dirty, unarmed combat and its mysteries were practice on hair mats in the gym, instructed by stout men who seemed to like wearing handlebar moustaches. For vital operational purposes the retaining of information till it became indelible was the main key. Jumping out of a plane in the night was practiced over and over with the use of landing codes. Anna and Robert relied on the tutors just as the tutors relied on the potential agents. The tutors had been tried in the field and had the ability to choose a person capable of taking in and using the skills taught. Time was of the essence as Germany would not wait for them to catch up, the Nazi regime would see to that. It was Anna how asked if Robert knew anyone other than Nazi supporters in the Reich. He couldn't help himself hesitating for a moment nor wanting to answer that question without giving it some consideration. Anna gave her most attractive look and pressed him further. Then he relented. "I knew a few, especially Americans they liked a good time as I did. One particular man was William Shirer a journalist who had lived in Europe for some time. I remember it was March 1938 when I was in Vienna when the Germans annexed Austria they called it the Anschluss. I was leaving Vienna for London by plane. That was where I met William on the plane; it was full of confused Jews leaving in a hurry. In London we talked a little and asked me to look him up, as the Americans say, when I returned to the Continent. He was then turning his talents to radio broadcasting along with the famous Edward Murrow's boys. British broadcasting was miles behind the times and began the banning of correspondents talking over the radio. William thought it was crazy and so did I. After his broadcast in London CBS changed their minds and did an about turn and allowed correspondents to use the radio especially in live broadcasts." Anna insisted he told his tutor of this important connection.

"This is an excellent discovery that may be of some use in the future so we have arranged for you to contact anyone you find relevant to our needs. Also we cannot give you a false name as you are known as Robert to so many Germans which may carry its own dangers, but it is better this way." The tutor rose from the chair and walked over to Robert and Anna and placed his hand on their shoulders. "It is near time to end training and begin preparations." He spoke quietly. "We have done our best to train you not only as spies but as saboteurs and couriers. Should you find yourself in a situation we have not covered use your natural cunning, it may surprise you. At this juncture in the war we need the best, so we now rely on you. Personally you have my vote and my admiration." At that he left the room to two very nervous novo agents. Robert felt Anna's hand in his and was thankful for it, feeling that they were in the same boat. Anna thought that they had been through difficult times but what was the point of digging up their past, dislikes or likes. They were in fact strangers on the same journey to an unknown netherworld.

Both were wined and dined by the Beaulieu staff with fresh game and fruits. Anna had her hair up to show off her lovely face. Her eyes were bright with the wine and candle light. Woolly had given instructions to the catering staff to make it an evening the youngsters would remember. Robert, next morning was called in to have a final word with Woolly. "We want you to go to Berlin as a civilian to continue your studies in a university being a doctor you will have a multiple of choices and to find an opportunity to reconnect with old friends; this will try to arrange in detail. Your prime objective is to intermingle and to find out as much as you can about everyday life in the city. This is basically an introduction to the field, giving you a chance to get the feel of it. If you do well we will give you another undertaking, but should you find something of the preparedness of the military, we would be very interested. It goes without saying this will be very risky indeed. We will in certain circumstances allow you to pick the targets. I take it you are fully prepared for the job in hand?" Robert now recognised he could be very useful with a bit of luck and lots of cunning. "Sir, I'm well prepared intellectually and physically. I'm very pleased you have given me this chance to show my capabilities in the spy world." Robert felt a tightening around his chest and his hands shake. The tutor smiled at Roberts's confidence. "Firstly we have to kit you out as a normal German gentleman with all the correct documents. Everyone knows of German fondness for being thorough in administration. Remember you cannot look too German or maybe you should. You decide as it's all about using common sense. A final brief then we send you to Bristol Whitechurch to fly to Lisbon then connect with a flight to Berlin. You will stay for two nights in Lisbon to get the feel of things. Portugal is of course neutral but it has its gathering of Germans on the lookout. This is an opportunity to find out what is happening in Berlin before you arrive. One more thing Robert I have spoken to the family of the Jewish man you say did not killed. They have not heard a word from him since the incident so they presume you killed him, but one thing they agreed in is you should be used to fight the Nazi's. Should you survive it is agreed you must return to face the family justice if the result is murder. It has been decided the family will be asked to choose what to do with you and whether you should be prosecuted or not. You must realise the importance of this. We thought it best to wait until you finished training before telling you, as you would have enough on your mind during that time." Robert nodded his head and then looked Woolly in the eye and answered. "I must do whatever it takes and then be brave enough to face my fate, I leave it at that. And will Anna be coming with me?" Robert had hoped this would be the case. "No that is not possible she has a completely different agenda. The only thing I will tell you is she will fly from this airstrip." Robert found himself missing Anna already; it must be like this for every operator, that isolation and dislocation of feelings from others.

When he saw Anna later he knew he was not allowed to say anything of his operation. He walked up to her and looked in her eyes to see that same lost look he had been carrying. He kissed her and was reward by her a warm response. The rest of the day they were inseparable hoping each minute would last an hour.

26.

History never knows how to say Goodbye.

But eventually Robert was called for the last brief and then departed. He unwillingly said his goodbyes to Anna. "I hope we are lucky and have an opportunity to see each other again in the near future and who knows." Anna only answered, "Yes who can tell?" He could hear her foot falls all the way down the corridor. Then he faced the silent wooden door that must have been at least a hundred years old. "Well this is it." He mumbled to the door and himself before grasping the door handle.

Bristol Whitechurch was busy with travellers that were under the eyes of an increasing number of security guards. There was an air of intense excitement while Roberts's nerves were fraught with worry. The flight to Lisbon an ancient port was as far as Robert could see was operated by a Dutch Airline. The plane waiting on the runway, much to his surprise was a brand new American Douglas Dakota. The fellow passengers were of all sorts, as business men and women with its share of conspirers that had some interest in Lisbon. Robert knew that the Prime Minister of that country walked an international tight rope having to deal with the each side of the war game. He had been warned of the Estado Novo the Portuguese version of the Gestapo who had the ability to make any person vanish without so much as a whisper in response. This made Robert realise that evil was on the move and spreading over the continent. His training was limited and he realised he could be talking to an enemy in polite conversation from day one. He closed his eyes and drifted to more pleasant thoughts as he flew passed barren mountains and seas of pillow clouds. To his surprise the flight went peacefully and was delightedly he was met not by just one person but a group of men and women. It seemed so natural meeting enthusiastic friends. One of the men embraced him whispering the code name 'Father and Friend.' The man was well dressed and appeared to be a business type. Robert along with the whisperer and an unknown woman drove off in a taxi to the Victoria hotel. The women was first to talk explaining that she would be his lover but would be staying in a separate room in the hotel; she gave the name Vivienne while correcting her lipstick in the murky image of the taxi window. Then she casually introduced him to Antonio as one of the leaders. Antonio was a dealer in gold and as such had some contact with members of the government. That was the sum of the conversation as the taxi came to a halt under the hotel lights. The next day he was to meet Antonio at Baixa a busy part of Lisbon with its myriad of streets and cafe's intermingled with the crowded shops. He could see it was the ideal place to meet and then vanish in the crowds. In a corner cafe Antonio told Robert he was an old friend of his father who had visited Lisbon many years before on holiday. They had become fast friends both interested in the possibility of making a fast buck. But that was in the past Antonio insisted. "The Germans were interested in gold and tungsten and were capable of any deed to get their grubby hands on both elements. You see, I have to do deals with them and the government to remain as neutral as the country. The cafe was far from being lively like the others Robert had seen on the way there. It was rather dim and one may be tempted to say grubby. "Look at the table next to the door but please do not stare." Antonio asked in a polite but assertive manner. Robert let his eyes trace the floor and then look up at the table.

Four men sat around in old clothes. Two had what must have been white trousers dark stained and ragged. The other two had coloured clothing creased and untidy. Their wine glasses remained untouched for long periods. Robert noted this as they lazily leaned on tired elbows and much of the few conversations they had were in low whispers. "They are the Estado Novo and this is their favourite cafe bar. No one on the run or new in the city would expect the police to frequent such a place. Informers know exactly where to contact them and where they must come to spend the reward money, as the Estado own the place. You see David, this wonderful vibrant country with its fine people who are now so corrupt. The Jews have come to Baixa to escape reprisal from the Nazis only to be robbed here. For a Jew to move anywhere abroad there are piles of paper work to complete and this done deliberately at a snail's pace, while they are gradually robbed of their wealth.

27.

Portugal Fell into the Magic Potion.

The poor people are the ones who will likely travel by ship chartered and funded by the American Jewish Joint Committee, with the help of the British and American embassies. As you can imagine there is a long tailback of vulnerable frightened people sleeping where they can in the dockyards and alleys. They are easy targets for the Police and others who see an easy prey. The rich that can afford the luxury of a prominent hotel and there they can wait patiently for a seat on the twice a week flying boat. Millions are here now at the first step to freedom and well mixed with a good share of spies and agents. Not exactly a healthy blend but the war has created it so. They are like the soup kitchens sprouting up all over the city, while feeding the needy show the weakness of civilisation. To make matters worse Portugal is the host of the World Exposition along the docklands which has massively intensified the crush of human driftwood". Robert asked to see some of the city and Antonio gladly agreed as he was glad of any excuse to get away from this place. As they were about to leave the cafe one of the police recognised Antonio and remarked. "Ha! Antonio we will be watching you and your guest." He then smiled and banged the table. The others burst into laughter also banging the table. Outside Antonio said jokingly, "Of course they will be watching me as I'm a very good source of income to them."

Robert leisurely walked the Praca do Comercio square admiring the statue of King Jose 1 on horseback crushing the rising snakes under hoof. Antonio told of the event in 1908 when two men assassinated King Carlos 1 in the square. Shots were fired from the crowd killing the King and mortally wounding Filipe the heir and hitting Prince

Manuel in the arm. The assassins were shot immediately by the royal body guards. The assassins were members of the Republican Party who came to power two years later. To Robert, this story stood as a reminder of the dangerous state of affairs in this changeable country.

They walked quietly to an opening to Augusta Street to another square called the Rossio. A half-moon came in to view just as the sun was backing behind the horizon of classic buildings. The street and square were silent and cool as some vibrant stars appeared steadily filling the late evening sky. A large tom cat walked past with a marked dignity as if it were the mayor of Lisbon, purring in the silences of that time of the day. Antonio explained the necessity of being in Lisbon as the world raged in war. Secret transactions worth millions and its close companion double dealing were commonplace. But the main capital was not so much money as the gathering of information. Antonio mentioned the SS had established a bank account for stolen gold, money and jewellery under the name of Max Heiliger in Switzerland. "We want to get our hands on that load before it disappears to South America. So we want to know what the Germans have in mind. What will be their next move and we don't want guesswork it must be real and factual." Robert agreed, but reminded Antonio he was here for only a few days. Robert stopped and put a hand on Antonio's shoulder and asked for advice. "I have to be in Germany soon and be convincing. I have to show I would die for their cause. How is that done?" Antonio looked Robert in the eye and spoke slowly. "You see my friend we all act throughout our lives in different parts daily, now is the time to convince your soul or die. There are no two ways about it, jump into the acting mode right now or I will be force to have London call the whole thing off. It may interest you that in Lisbon we have a British well known spy who dresses as a woman and everyone knows of his identity and we have another who gleams information from English tourist guides and sends them to the Germans, both have belief in what they do and have survived some time." Robert shivered and felt as dark as the streets were becoming. His soul was as dead as Timgad and as lonely as the other side of the moon.

Antonio had arranged for a taxi to take them to the Avenida Palace Hotel in the middle of Lisbon. The hotel stood out bathed in light featuring its fine building lines. Inside the bar was comfortable and busy; where they sat they could see the clientele drinking with great enthusiasm. The only word Robert could use to describe the persons in the bar was cosmopolitan. This was a hive of well-dressed people flirting around the tables where it seemed they all talked at once. After quick and satisfying refreshments they moved to the more sedate elegant sitting room with its high wonderfully stained glass ceiling and white pillars. A man not far was pretending to read the newspaper. Next was a young couple where the girl held hands with her lover while he read the evening paper avidly. Robert could hear an old gentleman between sips of drinks uttering "In 1927 I played Hamlet." A woman in black with a sorry looking hat remarked, "Have you played anything since? "The old gentleman responded. "Yes, my mother's old piano and did well playing the stock exchange where I'm considered to be a maestro." A German with white spats talked lazily of the importance of avoiding the doldrums of being penniless. The woman agent Robert had met on arriving called Vivien came into the room licking her red lips and with a photographic smile. It was a well-practiced smile aimed at destroying any resistance to her charms. He wondered what his chances might be and remembered his father's words, 'hope keeps more people alive than all the doctors ever born.'

Robert heard a thud close by and looked down on the floor and was surprised to see a silver pistol with an ivory handle. Those around did not seem in the least interested so he bent over and picked it up. He leaned over to ask a man nearest to where the pistol had fallen and asked, "Is this yours, sir?" The man was small wearing a silken hat. He almost jumped out of his seat when he saw the pistol. His face turned to blackness before he replied. "Good Lord, put that away before we are all arrested." Robert placed the pistol in his side pocked and left the room triumphantly liking the idea of having a weapon to defend himself in this assemblage of strangers. Sixty second later he was on the main street.

It was cosy under the main street lamp lights but when he left the lights the atmosphere changed to an uncomfortable lattice of shadows. As he turned a sharp corner a woman in an extravagant dress ran past nearly knocking him over while her perfume set his heart a flutter. He did not notice the shabbily dressed man till his arm was gripped vice like. It was the policeman he had seen earlier. "How would you like to end up in the river my friend?" "No I would not." answered a breathless Robert. He could just see the bunched fist snap towards him. His training took over and blocked the blow with ease. His elbow struck the policemen under the chin sending him against a brick building. The policemen spitting out blood hastily tried to reach for his gun but was surprised when Robert stuck a silver pistol in his gaping mouth. "I should have known you were one of those undercover men, the British create so skilfully." The policeman rose to his full height still spitting out blood from a hurt mouth. Before the policemen slouched away he whispered. "I would appreciate if you would keep this unfortunate incident from Antonio, he may stop my payments and I have a family to keep. That is why I followed you to demand you not to interfere with my business." "You have no worries on that aspect providing you give me a little information." Robert asked. Even in the covering darkness the policeman seemed to turn a little pale. Robert did not give him time to recover. "Is Antonio a double agent?" "This is Lisbon and everyone is playing dirty underhand games. Does that answer your question?" Robert then left the policeman who was still spitting blood.

The next day Robert felt better and enjoyed Antonio's company knowing he could not be trusted. He did wonder if Antonio knew anyway in this twisted game.

In the evening Vivienne appeared and made a fuss of Robert taking his arm to accompany him as if they were in a proper relationship. She was as tall as Robert with her blond hair fastened in a bun shape held together with a Spanish clasp. In her tight outfit with slim line skirts and gold buckled and her high heels. Her makeup always seemed to need attention or improving as if she were not beautiful enough. Robert would chat to her in a light hearted way on the Lisbon hills and bustling city while Vivienne made agreeable sounds and smiled. It was difficult for Robert to know if she was in the least interested. As the last evening began she told Robert she had been chosen to go with him to Berlin. "I thought it might be you anyway, how is your German?" asked a flattered Robert. Vivienne put her hand on his knee and leaned forward to kiss him on the cheek. Robert felt as a small boy at Christmas. He did feel however she was deadly confident and would make a formidable enemy and a trusted companion. She decided to play the part of his partner to the fullest extent and followed him to his room and bed.

He was a little sad to leave the magnificent hotel and its gentile appearance with the underlying current of deceit and corruption that surely awaited him. This he felt was a good beginning and had to admit he enjoyed the last two days especially the last night. This spy business in a foreign was like learning a complicated card game with many players where the losers lost their life. On Robert's last morning before midday flight to Berlin as he walked along an elegant corridor he was met by a well-dressed Egyptian. "My friend I have something to tell you and you must listen carefully. I was advised by Mohammad to contact you." Robert was taken aback thinking the Egyptian was at first after his money but that theory was dispatched at a glance as he could see he was neatly and expensively dressed. The man took out of his pocket an ivory snuff box and satisfyingly took a sniff. "I have travelled by air over much of the African continent for several years finding very little to interest me till seven weeks ago. I flew by chance over an old tomb unrecorded, but it looked like the resting place of a great being. The only mention of a burial in that area that I could find was made by Belzoni even then the information was very sketchy. It was written inside a book in Belzoni's small personal library I came across during an uninvited visit one night. The book was a copy of a diary by Howard Carter and the notes were inside the book sleeve. Many Egyptologists indeed visited the place and dug up the sands to no avail, there was a list of them. I asked the pilot to fly over it once more which he did and if possible find a safe landing place. From the pilots map I marked that place in case of some misadventure.

91

During our stay of two nights we were visited by tribesman who told us of grave robbers. They talk about ladies filling their skirts with fabulous jewels at the tomb not too remote from there. This was some twenty years ago but the tribesmen were struck down with a mysterious illness that took them to the arms of Allah. By the word of the tribesman ensured the Egyptian there are even greater riches and rewards to be found, but the desert sands are unrelenting with storm after storm covering any signs. The sun has baked the earth and crusted the surface so that the only marks to be seen are those of creatures that live here. The Egyptian took Robert by the hand and gave him the Carter Diary book cover pressing his fist tight to ensure he had a hold on it. Robert asked," Aren't you afraid the pilot will sell the information as soon as he can?" Taking his hand away the Egyptian then lifted two of his palms upward. "I shot him of course, what else could I do, wait until he betrays me? There are many pilots ready to take his place." Robert watched him slip away down to the banks of the river. He thought, why me, I may go my grave soon and to make matters worse I do not know the first thing about digging in the desert. After a few moments of deep thought, the idea of doing it by himself seemed logical and a confidence stole into his being. I trained to be a spy when I should be studying or teaching medicine, they are not exactly alike. He remembered the Tarot card of the hanging man that brought changes to the searcher. He asked himself again, haven't you noticed life is urging you on to new things you never dreamed of previously and he had to agree the world had been curiously different these few months. He ran his hand through his hair shuffled his feet and move off with a new found spring in his feet.

His main thoughts were of Vivienne and the important destination of Berlin. She was a dream come true and more, her strong personality made her an anchor. In the hotel he called for their suitcases to be sent down to the reception which were carried by a smirking young man. Robert noticed the locks on his case were scratched and meddled with. He quickly took the silver pistol from his pocket cocked it and slipped it into the pocket of the young smirking man. As he paid his bill and held polite conversation with the receptionist there was the sound of gun fire in the corridor. Robert and Vivienne picked up their suitcases and were about to leave the hotel when the man with the silk hat appeared and looked puzzled. "What on earth is going on?" he asked. "Someone has gone off half cocked" Robert answered as he went out the door.

Vivienne was puzzle but not surprised by the goings on of Robert who was stepping up to the job. She hoped one of them would survive the war and become rich this she had dreamed of during the last week. A week of dreams does not make a reality, she reminded herself. The future is a stranger even moments away and has to be embraced to be lived.

The airport was a busy anthill of those who were intent on leaving this beautiful city for whatever reason. Vivienne almost ran to keep up with

28.

Berlin is Like Being Abroad in Germany.

Robert as he reached the Berlin flight entrance. Robert looked around and took in the intense moment, in response he held Vivienne close and felt the uneasiness of the instant leave. She was soft and curvy with strands of steel entwined in her being enough to be relied upon in a given situation. But most of all she was lovely with those long eyelashes that women preferred and lips that cried out to be caressed. Her voice was soft as a warm zephyr on a summer morn. There could be no better companion to fly to Berlin with, to sit beside and smell her engaging perfume. Much better than the recent German newspapers that pedalled propaganda in all directions. In one page a new game was advertised as Stuka. It was like the Chinese checker game where the pegs had to be moved from one side of the board to the other without landing in the yellow which represented searchlights and the red where you were shot down. This was a game for children. The paper also advertised the Nazis published series of booklets intended for the youth of the country. They were titled the Kriegsbucherei der deutschen Jugend (War library for the German youth). These were war stories to encourage the youth to join up. In the half-light he saw the old buildings of Lisbon in his mind and felt its romantic attraction. He would rather have stayed with Vivienne and rid himself of this war. He shook the weakness of the notion away and settled to relax as best he could. The planes thundering props and occasional shudder retained the depth of his shallow sleep. A lady across the way fluttered her handkerchief and turned her head so that they looked into each other's eyes. It was a surprising comfortable feeling after all we are all human beings, he supposed.

The military man aboard sat upright as if to show their medals but far more revealing was the slight grim they had that covered a secret of some great victory yet to come. Was it Britain or more like the whole world under their whims that gave them that superior posture?

The cosy feeling of certainty fell like that of a barometer in response to foul weather when they crossed over the Bay of Biscay. As the aircraft tossed and bumped Robert rediscovered he was not an aeronautical lover and held on to Vivienne who looked happy and confident taking in the sights and noises as part of a wonderful adventure. Robert put on a set smile as if he was constantly pleased with the world and as he turned to a military man he wore the appearance of a clown. Many of those going on board were military men but this one was of a high rank and who had been examining both of them seriously. He didn't know the reason for the smile and presumed Robert was an idiot of sorts. But Vivienne had caught his interest and he felt a strong jealousy of Robert and frankly avoided Roberts's facial expressions, more of his attention was for Vivienne's long legs and film star appearances. He tried to attract her attention as best he could with warm smile that appeared to Robert as a sickly grin that belonged to a gorgon that had spent time under the elements. Robert nudged Vivienne and whispered in her ear that she had an admirer that looked like Hitler's brother. Vivienne looked over to her admirer her eyes glowing and her lips pouted as if in expectancy of a fond kiss. Von Kutcher had expected a response as he considered himself a ladies' man of some repute. He had never seen anyone so beautiful so perfectly made and shaped. She would make an ideal addition to his flat in Berlin and a prize others would love to have. He had not long completed training in the SS and as an already qualified doctor and had to admit he felt superior to his fellowman and a woman like this woman would doubtfully prove his lofty position.

Some of the passengers were smart business men with their vocal wife's chatting excitedly of their businesses and plans to make a fortune out of the war as long as it lasted. A large air hostess who had showed them to their seats reminded Vivienne of a large lizard with protruding eyes and exaggerated movements similar to a praying mantis. Her hair was tied up to make an anchor for her hat. She took note of each passenger and their places in the aircraft which Robert began to recognise as a German practice. On reaching the SS doctor she lowered her shoulders and whispered in his ear. Whatever it was Robert wanted to know. But he soon found it was Vivienne he had asked about. The lizard lady hostess leaned over Vivienne and asked her if she would like to move seats to sit by the SS man. She did not argue and rose to leave her seat without a word to Robert who was completely surprised. The SS man dismissed the man sitting next to him who marched to the other end of the plane and welcomed Vivienne placing his arm around her showering her with complements. Robert could hear only some of the conversation which was mainly about an apartment in Berlin. The SS man boasted about how easy it was to get domestic help as over a million were still employed as such Germany. Robert began to relax knowing Vivienne was only doing her job and relaxed sinking his back the shape of the aircraft seat. Most of the women in Britain in a domestic roll had left to work in the war factories or were beginning to join the services. He heard the SS man say some of the women were beginning to joining the searchlight batteries or the Flack Korps in case of eventual enemy bombing raids. Others were selling badges in the streets and organised special concerts to raise funds. Some were doing portrait sketches of passer-by's while the more military made money by inviting people to hammer a nail into a map of Britain. Robert could imagine the delight of some of the Germans hammering a nail into a city they have never seen nor probably ever see. He knew that contributions would be gathered in British in a more homely style such as organise jumble sales or garden fetes. The difference between the countries was in the ability of the people to listen to the radio. In Britain this was encouraged whilst in Germany listening to foreign programs was punishable by death. Being put to death for something you do in your own home in an ordinary day seemed alien to Robert and summed up a malevolent law.

The planes touched down and disembowel in the late evening as the rain came down in hails. Von Kutcher shared his umbrella with

Vivienne as they dashed towards his large black car with the SS emblems. Robert was not far behind splashing through the deepening puddles and feeling his shoes take in water. Kutcher stopped smartly and politely ushered Vivienne to the back seats where his valet helped her into the warmth and comfortable of the luxury vehicle. They had not wasted a minute since arriving at the airport. There was no clearing or waiting for luggage just an exchange of words which included the names of those who accompanied Kutcher. The airport staff snapped to attention and hurried with that frantic haste when the SS were present. In the car Vivienne introduced Robert as a Doctor and his quest to study tropical diseases in a German university. Kutcher studied Robert for a minute and asked why he wanted research tropical diseases, not a very popular subject in war time? Robert stretched his hand out shake Kutchers, which Kutcher willingly took. "The Reich is expanding to the west and in time will choose the east and that is where I come in. At least I will be part of a group already prepared for the new Germany." Kutcher was clearly impressed and his dislike and uncertainty disappeared. Tell me more of yourself Robert are you a Jew for instance? "Not likely." Vivienne interrupted he is wanted in Britain for killing a Jew. Robert cringed at this explanation that seemed so matter a fact and inhuman. This was his ace card and despite his reluctance he knew it this kind of sickening act opened doors for him. "You will be thoroughly checked by the Gestapo and the SS. But till then I will show you some Berlin hospitality. Kutcher took them to his apartment and made them welcome. He phoned his many friends and organised a get together to celebrate his return. "There will be twenty of us Robert and how many bottles of whisky do you think we need." Not wanting to appear mean Robert contemplated a large number. "How about three dozen that should keep everyone happy and there might be others that will drop in." "Excellent." Kutcher remarked as he picked up his phone. "And how many bottles of Champaign will be needed for those who prefer a more sophisticated tipple." Kutcher asked in a sarcastic manner. Robert rose to this and demanded another three dozen bottles of the best in Berlin.

29.

The Gestapo Officers and Chess.

Robert stood at the door with Kutcher and shook hands with the German high ranking SS and Gestapo men and women. He smiled at them all giving a hearty welcome and a glass of whisky. At first he thought he wasn't sure if he knew any of them and later he might know some of them and a bit later he was sure he knew some of them well. Such was the power of a good whisky they began to chatter lightly and them in turn to a thunderous roar with faint music in the far back ground. The room was a maze of personalities laughing and attempting to hug the centre stage. Robert made jokes of subjects he would never have dreamed of and made the company laugh loudly. His first discovery was they were not all German, some from Poland and others from further east all spoke good German with the exception of the American. Europe He tried to re member their names and position in the Reich by tagging them. Alder became older and Beike became bike and Blau as windy with the aptly named Aderlasser the blood letter. The party began to have a will of its own moving from crude to wild and wilder. Vivienne and the other ladies appeared softening the atmosphere and transformed the will argue to dance to the waltz tunes of Vienna. Robert forgot his gathering of information and raced to reach Vivienne before another beat him. He held her tight as they swayed across the room seeing the expressions of envy from the company.

When Robert opened his eyes he found the fog of war had entered his brain. He turned his head to the side to see the alarm clock and found it gone from its usual place. It was a large fancy clock that would not have been out of place in the palace of

Versailles, but it was not on the bed side cabinet. Robert with great effort lifted himself up and gazed across the floor, there the clock lay with a bullet hole in its face. Vivienne lay near the clock and Robert thought he might have shot her as well as the clock. The hangover was a classic radiating across his head like a fierce bundle of mad red devils. Each one determined to destroy his thoughts and vision not forgetting his balance. The mirror of the cabinet had red lipstick marks that resembled a large heart with a circle in the middle that was surely a grin. Curtains that covered the long window had been set on fire and had burned the curtains and ceiling black. The phone was in the toilet with the earphone hanging over the side, the telephone directory was in the bath with some pages stuck up the cold and hot taps. How on earth he thought, could one person cause so much damage it was more like the aftermath of a war party of an apache raid. Vivienne was barely conscious and crawled to the bed and with a super effort threw herself on to it swearing never to leave it again. Robert felt the same but he heard the door bell and wondered towards it dreamily. Six burley men in raincoats looked at Robert amazed a human being had allowed himself to deteriorate to this level. "Get dressed quickly your presence is required at Prinz-Albrecht-Strasse." Robert knew this was the Gestapo Headquarters and agreed at once to hurry. His mind was a bowl of spaghetti wiring all terminals firing in the wrong order. The alternative was death by torture or shooting so with all his guile he dressed himself in a fashion. The Gestapo men were too busy studying the splendid anatomy of Vivienne as she laid semi naked across the bed as she moved in her sleep unconsciously displaying one of her magnificent breasts. He could have run out the door and they would not have noticed and returned with a German military band and they would have continued their fantasies without blinking. Robert was about twenty minutes in dressing and the Gestapo seemed unconcerned. "Come on I have a date at your headquarters." He said, shaking a little. Their superior took out a packet of cigarettes and offered one to Robert." He took it gladly as a sign of benevolence and as his hand reached out the Gestapo man asked him who was the fortunate man to have Vivienne as a lover? Robert mumbled, Kutcher. "That bastard, I thought so, watch out he would kill you without a murmur of conscious for as little as a broken penny whistle." "For a girl like that he would slit his grannies throat and sing while he did it." "Come, time is being wasted on the living." It may have been the shower of rain but Berlin although busy had a covering of grey even the trees next to the HQ had lost their green. Robert thought trees covered a multiple of evil as they spread out towards the light while just across road a German hell sustained a multitude of torments. He pulled physically through the large door and along an endless corridor to a wide space room. All ranks including a Field- Marshall moved around in the space appearing to be unconcerned about the intermittent screams and some played chess. A heart rendering female shriek filled Roberts's heart and he wished the jokes of yesterday would be forgiven by a sympathetic God. He knew that if the shriek had been done by Vivienne he would have lost his grip and shot them all. So much he thought, for out thousand years of civilisation. The room had a smell of furniture polish and a faint whiff of bleach rendering the place neutral to human odours. A smartly dressed group of four Gestapo looking as if they were on the way to a funeral sat around a table. "My name is Albench." Said, the one with the fancy soft white hat, so sure of his superiority he banged the table top so hard it juddered. "It's like this; the parties aim is the law and is absolute without recourse. Do you understand?" Robert answered as quietly as he could to give the illusion he was completely unafraid. "Violence is not a hobby." Albench stated with a short burst of laughter. "Or maybe it is?" A newspaper lay next to the waste bin, the headline read Nazi Egyptologists found dead in the desert. One survived and is now in care for the insane. He had babbled about blood on the ground. No one could make any sense of his remarks. The Egyptian and German police have written the incident off as a case of murder by an insane man. Robert knew that one of Hitler's dreams of world domination had come to its end by strange bacteria. Robert wondered if Hitler would have used the microorganism for good, but he had his doubts as his record so far was far from showing unwilling to help anyone bar himself. Robert pulled himself together and made himself look interested in what Albench was saying. But under it all he was relieved and could now put the Egyptian incident behind him.

30.
Illusions and Russia.

Cameron sent for Molina as the summer had come upon England at last and the best of the season with all its glory settled on the land and sea. They were both glad to see each other, both stealing glances at every chance to reassure themselves they were near to each other. Molina wanted to know what Cameron had been doing, although she had read all of his articles in the newspapers and was updated with the war, what she truly wanted to hear him speak and touch his body. She wanted details of his feelings of the war and of France and any other swan he had become involved in. He had evoked a sense of adventurism and that was the reason she associated the word swan for his reports of the war. The trees lush leaves rusted gently in a warm breeze and combed the grass on the hill they had chosen for a picnic. Molina was happy as she had ever been wading in a comforting bliss. Whereas Cameron wanted to shout out his joy and sing a song like the morning birds and tried to make a joke of everything to make her happy. There was nothing in the world he liked better that see her wonderful face light up in laughter.

They exchanged details of their friends and in the service of their country and felt them near to them. Although in truth they had no real idea of where they were at that moment in time. They should be safe and sound in this world full of tyranny. Cameron was given his mission as a war correspondent and had chewed it over till he had accepted its risks and rewards. The public had a right to know the truth of the events in this war and he would be instrument in relaying it from the point of contact to the publishing. He had awoken in the wee small hours and thought deeply of his choice which he now accepts, as in war time refusing an appointment was to send other in you place. This he knew he could not do and live with. It would be difficult to carry on his life knowing he had sent another into the fight while he was safe at home. The sun and the rain would be different and life almost alien and his heart would belong to the word no and its everlasting consequences. Cameron had waited till he could speak to Molina of his dilemma. He made up his mind in an instant he saw her even knowing he may never see her again, he would fight for her. Any doubts no longer lingered knowing he would be afraid but he would just have to get used to it. Russia was a strange country so often our enemy in the past. He had been chosen to make a report on the readiness of that country to face the German might, if they decided to attack. German mischief was in the air with straws in the wind indicating an invasion eminent, or was it part of Hitlerism and the ability to fool the other side. He was to make his way to Russia by whatever means necessary and that meant some risk.

He explained to Molina of the growing number of Russians on the borders near Germany. "The average soldier had his head crammed of ideology and changes in an army that sometimes led a company or unit to just go home whenever they chose. The Bolsheviks after the revolution had remade the army as different as the imperial army as possible. The Bolsheviks had recruited as best they could from the Red Army, workers, keen party members and plentiful peasants in a voluntary force. Stalin had reversed the voluntary side but in time changed his mind as he often did. The order of the day by Stalin (the man of steel) was not to provoke and incident with the Germans who were also in the process of a build-up pretending it was for some other purpose.

Cameron remembered that time was passing quickly as the couple walked along a chalk stream and watched the trout dart from shadow to shadow. The sun appeared in waves of light and warmth through the tree canopy leaves, as they made their way down stream. They loved each other in the shades of the embankment that formed a moss and grass place to lie in comfort. Molina thought it was a paradise away from the world of trouble, secluded and safe to show emotions and passions. A pigeon flew wildly from the lower branches of a near tree and woke Cameron from a living dream. It battered its way out to the blue sky and flew upwards spiraling as its wings found the power to fly. He knew he would also have to leave here and fly to another destination. The six days he had of leave had been mainly occupied with Molina, being in her presence was enough to please him and made his dreams a reality.

31.

The Mills of God grind slowly.

It was nearly one year since the vengeful Germans made the shattered French sign their surrender in the forest of Compiegne. Some of the Government though Hitler's triumphs were now complete after a series of impressive victories. Cameron sat in the plane slightly uncomfortable. Not only for the leaving of Molina but for the uncertainty of his next journalistic remit. He knew that the postponing of Operation Sea Lion the German high command had another victim in view. The supply route attack over the rolling Atlantic was an indirect blow to the British but Hitler wanted a more powerful direct knockout blow. So far there was no move to attack Britain so where would the next blow take place. Hitler had been drawn into Mussolini's invasion of Greece and the German/ Soviet relationship had become strained.

Cameron sent for Molina as the summer had come upon England at last. They were both glad to see each other, both stealing glances at every chance. Molina wanted to know what Cameron had been doing, although she had read all of his articles in the newspapers. She wanted details of his feelings of the war and of France and any other swan he had become involved in. He had evoked a sense of adventurism and that was the reason she used the word swan for reporting the war. The trees leaves rusted gently in a summer breeze and pushed the tall grass as if combing the hill they had chosen for a picnic. She was happy as she had ever been and realised her presumed bliss was wanting. Whereas Cameron wanted to shout out his joy and sing a song like the morning birds. He tried to make a joke of everything to make her happy, there was nothing in the world he liked better that see her wonderful face light up in humour.

The exchanged details of their friends and families and felt them near although in truth they had no real idea of where they were at that moment in time. They were safe and sound and the world was full of optimism. Cameron had been given his mission as a war correspondent and had chewed the cud of indecisiveness. Waking up in the wee small and thought deeply of his choices which were accept or not. In war time refusing an appointment was to send other in you place. This he knew he could not do and live with and carry on his life as normal. The sun and the rain would be different and the face of his friends almost alien. His very heart would belong to that moment of decision if he said no. Cameron had waited till he was in the presence of Molina before he decided. The balance of thought would be weighed with more precision with her being close. He made up his mind in an instant knowing he may never see her again and the man he would become if he said no. The word, no, would linger on and on, yes would be fear he would just have to get used to. He would do it to help the country and by doing so help her continue to exist. He was to make his way to Russia and report without favour the Russian stance to Hitler's constant threats and war schemes.

He explained to Molina of the growing number of Russians on the borders near Germany. "The average soldier had his head crammed of ideology and changes in an army that sometimes led a company or unit to just go home. The Bolsheviks after the revolution had remade the army as different as the imperial army as possible. The Bolsheviks had recruited as best they could from the Red Army, Workers, keen party members and plentiful peasants in a voluntary force. Stalin had reversed the voluntary side but in time changed his mind. The order of the day was not to provoke and incident with the Germans who were also in the process of a build-up.

France had fallen in record time to the astonishment of the world and to the amazement of Fleet Street. Now as Cameron sat slightly uncomfortable in the plane his wish was he could have stayed with Molina a little longer and overcome the uncertainty of the Russian remit. He knew that the postponing of Operation Sea Lion the invasion of Britain the German high command had another victim in view could it be where he is going. The supply route attacks over the rolling Atlantic were an indirect blow to the British food and war supplies, but Hitler wanted a more powerful direct knockout blow. The RAF had in a few months upset Goring and his leader by standing up to the might of the Luftwaffe in a mix of luck and determination. An episode of pure German conceited that bordered on a fancy so swollen by victory that the next step led to a slip that changed the fortunes of the world. The world now looked on Germany no longer unbeatable but susceptible to a force of arms. Due to this miscalculation there was no move to attack Britain, so where would the next blow take place. Hitler had been drawn into Mussolini's invasion of Greece and the German/ Soviet relationship had become strained.

I'm used to meeting a lot of people in Berlin I attended nearly all the rallies as a youngster." The captain looked astonished and said, "Your Robert, I remember you at the burning of books. My name is Harvey do you not remember me. You were a star for a while in Berlin and may still be to those who remember the rallies." The lizard like woman asked the passengers to go to their seats and fasten their safety belts. Just before Harvey hurried to his seat he put his hand on Roberts shoulder and said. "I'm a man of business myself so keep in touch." Robert thought the opposite and would try his best to keep out of his way. In response he looked up at Harvey and nodded. There was a heightening of mumbles by the passengers as the aircraft flew into a dense cloud before breaking out into the dark blue evening sky. The plane then shuddered as it hit a rising of air Robert thought the vibrations were enough to shake the wings off. Robert felt Vivienne's hand slid into his and he felt braver than he had a minute ago; with her hands in his made the rest of the flight a joy. As the plane came into land its wings tipped and almost touched the ground but at the last moment the pilot managed to bring the wings to the horizontal. The passengers remained silent as if in shock and only broke that silence when they were sure the planes wheels were secure on the runway. When the plane taxied to the unloading area conversation returned mostly about the line of police whose eyes were fixed on the planes doorway. Roberts's instinct was to mix with a crowd and engage in the conversations as they left the plane. Many including Robert began to lit up a cigarette and at the same time offered one to Vivienne, who did not reply. She was casually studying the line of police hoping to recognise one. Robert stumbled as he tried to light his cigarette and dropped the packet on the ground. The key he had placed in his wallet hit the ground and travelled to the foot of a police officer. Vivienne put her hand over her mouth to signal Robert to say quiet. "I'm not quite ready to give a gentleman my key yet even if he is as handsome as you." She purred and smiled. The policeman was a drab man in his forties who suddenly became animated at the attention of a beautiful woman. He hurriedly picked up the key and cigarettes dusted them and handed them to Vivienne. "Madam I will always be at your service." He was trembling at his own confidence. "How gallant you are sir." Vivienne took the packet and strode off frightened of over doing the thank you bit. Going through the customs was eerie as the usually chatty officers were under the eye of the police. "I'm here on medical business hoping to find a permanent position in the great German Reich." "Then good luck sir." The customs officer replied. Robert and Vivienne sat in silence watching the others come through the customs gantlet. A young lady was made to open her baggage. The customs officer called over a policeman who dragged her away. She screamed so loud it filled a large open building. Two other policemen appeared and hit the woman with their batons to silence her. "The key is valuable if anything happens to me give it to my sister." Vivienne knew this was not the time to be seen whispering in public and loudly asked if he was hungry as she would love a sandwich of cheese with lots of butter. Vivienne using body language signalled him to hide the key quickly before setting off to find a place to eat. The wine was perfect and worked its wonders by loosening the tongues of the crowd. They became jolly and a few came over to exchange a joke or two.

Robert realised that was one thing they missed out on in training and that was a German joke. But he held is sides and pretended to be heartily amused. In a way the gathering of people in the lounge was remarkable with industrialists and military personnel mixing with watchmakers and electricians. It was a sign of the times when workers and bosses got together to defend the Reich in the way they saw fit. "Steady there. Don't push." Cried a police sergeant as a new German bride appeared and caused a surge of woman on to the scene. One of the women pushed the sergeant abruptly she shouted. "Officer, could you not move aside just a little." The sergeant was a big man but knew he had met his match and did so. That same woman grabbed her husband and ordered. "John can't you move your fat self?" The sergeant caught the mood and laughed at poor John being forced to move. He turned to the sergeant and said. "I'm only a little guy with a powerful wife; can you blame me for not answering back?" The sergeant agreed with him as the last thing he wanted was to be on the other end of her tongue.

32.

He alone, who owns the youth, gains the Future.

A hand rested on Roberts shoulder. In response he turned to see an SS officer. The officer named Jaeger asked them to follow him to their accommodations. They were we placed near the centre of Berlin in a small family hotel. Accentually it was more of an extended house with seven bedrooms, a lounge and dining room. At one end of the lounge a flag was prominently placed and close to it was a radio that blasted out German marshal music. The proprietors were Gerard and his wife Erica with a thirteen year old daughter Angeline and Egbert the ten year old son. They were blond and slim so unlike many Germans Robert has seen in his travels. Gerard had fought in the last war against the Highland Light Infantry and was wounded in 1915. Since that time he and his wife had built up the business. Times had been difficult not only for trade but due to a new system of spying on a neighbour and reporting to the Gestapo. A complaint be about a Jew would be investigated with full vigour. With the inevitable result of immediate imprisonment or execution even plain murder. Gerard explained this to Robert and Vivienne as he took them on a tour of the guest house to serve as a warning. The rooms were neat and tidy with clean linen on every bed and furniture free from dust. The sunlight of the evening gave the rooms a gentile and restful impression unshaken by events outside. Robert noticed a door move involuntarily and swung it open. He was surprised to find Egbert crouching behind the door smiling. Gerard asked Robert and Vivienne to sit down after sending Egbert away. "Egbert has just joined the Deutsches Jungfolk and is completely enchanted by them;

he enthusiastically complies with anything they asked him to do. This will include spying on his family and any guest in the house. Gerard despised this happening but could do little to change Egbert's mind. Erica was certain he would never do such a thing it was surely a trend he was going through trying to impress the Jungfolk and his new friends.

She reminded Gerard of the marches through the town with drums beating and Egbert marching proudly amongst the youth. The evenings after long route marches were spent sitting around the camp fire singing songs of Germanys growing power. Erica could only see how her lonely son had now become popular with other children and that was good enough for her. Looking over the dining room Robert was amazed at the quality of the table and chairs. The pictures on the wall were mainly country scenes and still life all situated in a place to show off their artistic value. The bed was comfortable and the service first class. Vivienne had decided she was to be Robert's wife and secretary to avoid complications. Robert offered very little resistance to this idea which worked well especially in the morning when Jaeger arrived very early to see Robert. Jaeger apologised for the early interruption but considered it important they knew a certain person who wished to talk with them. Robert felt his mood change as this information may lead to something worthwhile. He remembered Berlin as a busy sprawling city and the thought almost unnerved him. But Vivienne could feel his disquiet and placed her arms around him. It was a sunny morning when they left their accommodation and children were everywhere some on their bicycles racing ahead of their parents. One mother was aghast as her son rode his bike while paying little attention to where he was going. The bike front wheel hit a stone with such a force it send the rider flying on to the busy road. Robert wasted no time and ran to lift the boy clear. "Thank heaven you were here I just stood feeling helpless." Robert held the woman's hand and said, "Maybe this will teach the boy not to speed and to look where he is going. Please understand boys at his age are naturally careless this included myself a rascal and just as silly." The woman had a black coat heavy for this time of year and could only conclude she was cold and poor. He knew that soon the winter of war will bite and many more will suffer.

Some dust flew in the morning air and flickered in the rising heat. A white dog lay at the entrance of the address they were given by Jaeger and Robert a dog lover called it over. "Its name is Alex after his home town of Alexandra." Robert looked in the shade of the door entrance to see a smiling man he thought as tall as a lamppost with cheeks like a fat baby over a row of spiky teeth. "Allow me to introduce myself, my name is 'Alder and sometimes called the eagle." Vivienne was sure the name eagle was given for his ability to catch his prey. Vivienne knew the first night in Berlin had passed safely and now all that was needed was their chance to meet the right people. "This way please." instructed Alder. They could feel coolness in the lobby air as they walked behind. The person they were to meet was far from any they had imagined. She sat in comfy leather studded green seat smiling with rose bud lips. She wore a yellow woollen hat with grey trousers and out of her pocket perfect white handkerchief. "Amara is my name and I will explain what is expected of you." She pressed an old hotel bell that sounded as if it were on its last legs. A Middle aged man adorned with medals limped into the room. He had a walking stick with a lion's head that could easy be used as a weapon. His heals clicked and swung a right arm high in the Nazi salute. Robert took a second to respond and return the salute and Vivienne followed. The Middle aged man appeared satisfied of their response. He then called over his right shoulder and a small crowd came into the room bowing their heads and gave the Nazi salute. He recognised many of them as they approached him trying to remember when he last saw them. Soon they settled down to common gossip and old tales. "We remember you Robert and the day you came skiing or was it hurtling down the bowl near Obersdorf or was it Fellhorn/Kleinwalsertal where you over took Germany and flew into Austria. We watched you with binoculars and could just keep up with you." "Ah! But Dorf can you remember my month stay in hospital with a broken leg." Robert added. "Yes we can with all those pretty nurses succumbing to your every wish." "If only half of that was true my friends. My nurse was as big and broad as the town library building. And she was a sweet as a rhino on a bad day." "I remember you Carl," Robert said pointing to the youngest man there. "With two lovely blond girls sitting in an old carriage that went clack click, clack click in the shallow snow, you told me they were your Nannies and expected me to believe it. One of them was shocked at your remark and slapped you on the mouth." Carl replied, he married her the next year and have two wild boys. "An excellent excuse to celebrate all our good fortunes, shouted Robert enthusiastically." A loud chorus ensued and as they made their way happily to the drinks pool.

Robert felt at home and could believe most of the change as good news for Germany. He was taken through large doors all embossed with golden eagles and everywhere pictures of Adolf Hitler. "Come this way and meet our Commander Valken" A thin man politely asked. "Yes of course it shall be an honour." Robert said humbly. They are taken into a room of artistic beauty. Every object seemed very valuable and at the far ends of the room large desks with gold cigarette cases and ashtrays. There was a horse in pure gold rearing with its rider waving a six gallon hat. Robert was staring at the objects and forgot to look straight ahead. Commander Valken could see Roberts's reaction and gave a little laugh. "Hello," he said. "Robert you have been sent here to work under instruction from High Command. We can talk later, now I want you to be shown around and then to see your office you will be working from. You will then be told of your assignment." Robert saluted sharply and is given a warm smile from the Commander. Robert was led away and found himself intrigued by this place and the people in it. No one spoke as they enter a small lift. They are taken down 4 floors when the lift stopped and the doors opened. The place is dreary compared to the ground floor but there is plenty of light and air. There were no pictures just walls of grey paint. All the doors they pass are closed and little could be heard of people speaking. They were led into a room of mostly men working on radios where he could almost feel the Hertzian waves superseding the buzz of solenoids and the stifling feel of a room with no forethought for beings only the machines.

Robert and Vivienne could hear the Germans relay the plan for attacking the Netherlands. By breaking its resistance within a short space of time would enable them to free troops for operations in Belgium and France. Rotterdam was vital to this plan. What they didn't know was the city could have been captured with the minimum resistance on May 13th and May 14th. The garrison commander of the city received two ultimatums stating he should surrender the city or it would be destroyed.

German radio infrastructure between the air command and ground troops was often very poor. In May 14th Stuka bombers bombarded German tanks in a communications error in the Ardennes. This kind of failure was noted by General Kesselring as that failure of communications at the critical moment of battle was an everyday phenomenon. The use of light signals fired by ground troops on the southern banks of the river Mass would lead the aircraft to Rotterdam. Less than half of the aircraft saw the signals. The hesitation to bomb immediately was the work of the German army command, who hoped to keep the city of Rotterdam intact. A lie was communicated saying that British troops were landing on the Dutch coast giving an excuse to bomb the city at will. Within a short time the centre of the city was engulfed in a sea of flames. The next move would be the destruction of France. They watched in dread and admiration as the events unfolded.

Geordie had formed a few friendships in London one of them was the famous author Hector Bywater. They both were fond of good food if you could find it. The clubs and restaurants they found most favourable were those frequented by foreigners. Hector had noticed an influx of Russian and Japanese; they tended to be well dressed in pinstriped suits and favoured corner tables. By chance Geordie noticed when their eyes met the Russians peered back while the Japanese looked away. Hector often told stories in a loud voice and enjoyed others company and willingly allowed diplomats of some county or other to join the conversations. One of the stories was of Felix the cat that was officially on the Government staff in Whitehall. His pay was one penny a day and being a civil servant had rules to obey. Felix according to Hector had to keep himself clean while hunting for rats and mice. The cat was allowed to have a family but had to look after them by himself. The cat had ancestors to ancient times and should till this day anyone kill it they were to pay a fine. In the olden times they had to give enough wheat to cover the cat's body, why wheat and the covering of the body he couldn't tell, and as for today's fine he could only guess it to be £5. We never sure of the validity of Hectors tales, anyway with a few drinks it didn't matter.

Hector had written an astounding book away back in 1925 on The Great Pacific War. It Predicted the Japanese attacking the United States Naval Forces in the Pacific and was highly regarded by some and totally ignored by many. The book held several good pointers for President Roosevelt in countering Japanese moves in the Pacific in the 1930s. It was one of Geordies favourite books but he was not surprised at the author's expertise and prophetic abilities. Hector covered the Russian-Japanese War of 1904 and had served Britain before the First World War and as an intelligence officer and during it. He was familiar with the theories and conspiracies of the time. It was thought the Japanese Admiral Isoroku Yamamoto had studied the book and was prepared to use the tactics in the event of a war. When Hector was younger he was a foreign correspondent for the New York Herald and being a Welshman at heart he enjoyed life to the full and liked to tell of his exploits on his return to America his adopted country. In 1915 there had been suspicious happening in the New York docks where Irish and German conspirators were using sabotage to block the sea aid to Britain. There Hector averted a bombing plan by the Germans which would inevitably have caused panic in the then neutral United States. Geordie was on the way to visit him on a wet august day his mind was full of unanswered questions he would ask. This first would be Hector's ability to pass as a real German in language and style also how he gained the information the Japanese would forbid the fortification of Guam and the Philippines. Geordie encountered outside his friends door a policeman who informed him Hector had died of a heart attack or poisoning. He wasn't sure which. Geordie listened to the hospital doctor attribute Hectors death to

115

alcoholism. He knew this was nothing but pure fiction and waited the result of a post- mortem. But the post-mortem never took place as Hector was hurriedly cremated. In his mind Geordie the affair had been confusing and undetermined. The famous correspondent and naval expert was written off as casual as swapping a fly.

On the 19th may 1940 the PM Winston Churchill made his first radio broadcast.

"Today is Trinity Sunday. Centuries ago words were written to be a call and a spur to the faithful servants of Truth and Justice: 'Arm yourselves, and be ye men of valour, and be in readiness for the conflict; for it is better for us to perish in battle than to look upon the outrage of our nation and our altar. As the will of God is in Heaven, even so let it be."

Geordie back in Britain had received a phone call on the German attacks on the five radar stations between Dover and the Isle of Wight. When Geordie arrived he discovered only one was seriously damaged but recognising the danger to London the repairs were hurriedly carried out. He found himself a place to sleep near a telephone. Nearly asleep he heard a phone ringing it resounded through the station. It was the panic button again. Geordie understood the German tactics of drawing the RAF to fight over the channel and was not surprised on hearing the three forward airfields in Kent and the part of the Thames estuary had been attacked. He was tired and wanted a chance to get some sleep. When the phone rang and an orderly shouted, 'waken up sir, waken up sir.' He struggled to find his feet and make his way to the "We have picked up enemy planes about 110 miles away HQ No11 Group air defences had been tracking them. Fighter command turned away the enemy but an attack from the south had damaged southern ports but most important of all was damage done to the airfields. This time, Geordie thought, we were lucky, he knew it would be partly to faulty information given to the Germans. Fighter Commands airfield was fortunately missed and the jubilant radio message was 'Results very good.'

33.

The Uncomfortable amnesia of France, 1940.

The Mechelen Affair occurred in Belgium on January 10th 1940, a German aircraft carrying the plans for Fall Gelb (Case Yellow), which was the German attack on the Low Countries on certain dates. But the Germans became aware of the incident so when the dates came and passed the crisis abated. Most of the countries that felt threatened now relaxed while others were forewarned. Clearly the Germans had altered their plans to some extent but they still were intent on the invasion.

Robert had managed so far. He had brought some knowledge of medical advances to Britain. He knew that the Germans were great scholars and had to train harder than most countries and may be because of their extra efforts were more advanced. His reputation and eagerness had convinced them of his wanting to be one of them. He was sure at this point in time he did want to be part of this national pride. Keeping an eye out for any secret that might help Britain was part of his remit and contradicted this part of his being. But somehow like all plans had gone astray and they were here at with the German High Command. Vivienne and Robert began to it as they were young and enjoyed the party life. And the lightening campaigns where the German Army routed Poland. France and Britain had been like rest of the world astonished.

Cameron and Geordie were once again in France on hearing rumours of a German build up near the Low Countries borders. It seemed incredible that Fort Eben-Emael would fall so quickly. Its massive defences penetrated by 89 German airborne forces that landed on the top fortress by gliders. Using explosives and flamethrowers to disable the outer defences then entering the fortress and the garrison of 2,000 surrendered. Meanwhile the three bridges over the Canal were taken with heavy casualties by the paratroops and held until the German ground forces arrived. Both forces attacked the fort and forcing its surrender. Two of the bridges over the Canal were used to bypass Belgium positions and set forward the invasion. By attacking the Low Countries could outflank the Maginot Line and slice through Belgium into Northern France. And by exercising this movement cut off the British Expeditionary Force and the large France Army forcing them to surrender en mass. Rotterdam fell and the Germans met stern resistance at Ypenburg airbase where 11 German transports were shot down out of a total of 13. At Ockenburg airbase the German transports landed on the soft sand dunes near the base. Their job was to follow the events of the French army and report back to London. They thought this was a great idea and so different from the normal occupation of a British war Correspondent.

Cameron and Geordie were with French General Maxime Weygand who explained he had only 60 divisions against 130 German divisions 10 of those were armoured. He knew only one conclusion was possible in the hopeless situation. General Maurice Gamelin of the French Army also saw the hopelessness. Weygand wanted to save our honour. He knew what might happen. "The army must resist firmly in the Somme-Aisne and when this resistance was broken the fragments must stand fast to the end." Cameron and the rest of the HQ waited the War Council's solution to the ever increasing problem. Their idea was to form a line either to the left or the right and stop the German flood. It meant also the line would take in the Maginot Line or abandon it. Weygand dismissed the other proposal of withdrawing to the Seine-Marne Line. He put this down to "Because of the lack of reserves to carry out an orderly retreat." In the circumstances he felt it better to stand and fight. "It may crumble but each part of the Army must fight to the end." On May the 26th in his General Order he wrote, the fate of the country will depend on it being fought on our present position, without thinking of withdrawals. All leaders down to the platoon leaders must be imbued with the fierce desire to fight to the death. Geordie knew that some of the forces had already surrendered and not everyone would fight to the death. But wondered what would happen next. What would be the German plans?

There was only one way to go and that was towards the Channel.

A mass that grew to a stream of drifting humanity pushing past burning houses and vehicles in some hope of safety. The German bombing at will interrupted the human flow causing panic to the civilians and military alike. Cameron and Geordie were ordered to make the most of it and try to escape the German advance. Quickly they gathered what they could and left on an old truck full of just as old equipment. Shells burst in all directions with pieces of shrapnel landing on the canvass roofing. A deadening thud and the truck went left and then right coming to a stop slowly. The driver had been struck on the side of his head with one eye hanging out swinging around in the night winds. Cameron grasped the map and they fled into the dark, only to find the map was so blood-stained it could not be read. They moved mostly in the dark and constant shelling caused them to drift towards Dunkirk near the Belgium border. During the slog through the mud avoiding the actual roads they heard the sound of track vehicles. Geordie put his hand on Cameron's shoulder and whispered, "It's our tanks." Both in their enthusiasm threw caution to the winds and climbed on all fours over the thick grass clumps and jumped on to the road. A panzer swung around a broken down lorry that was still aflame. It was then they realised their danger and threw themselves head first back into the grass and mud. It was night before they moved on with that extra caution brought on by a fright. There was little conversation between them except at each junction where they decided which way was the safest to go. When they finally arrived on the Dunkirk beaches it was only French forces to be seen. Geordie guessed the date to be the 4th June. Cameron pulled Geordie with him to see a British Naval officer who appeared to be organising the crowds. He explained he had been ordered by General Weygand to escape the advancing Germans. The Naval Officer was satisfied with Cameron's explanation after he was shown their credentials as a War Correspondent. Cameron could see from the ship there were many French soldiers left behind. Time had run out for them.

More important, what would Weygand do with a depleted force. The General gave orders to form 'hedgehogs' and to install them in the woods and villages with the 75-mm guns to be used as anti-tank weapons. They resist would resist with honour before being overwhelmed. The Fuhrer announced to the world by radio, "The second great offensive is starting today with formidable new resources." Weygand appealed to the French to stand firm. Added, that the future of our children depended on your firmness'. On June the 7th Rommel avoiding the hedgehogs pushed over open ground and by the end of the day had reached 25 miles from the Seine at Rouen. A counter attack proved to be worthless and the 51st British division was cut off. The Commander in Chief Paul Baudouin who had served in the French Artillery during the Great War received a telephone message from Colonel Bourget that a tactical accident occurred and that the Panzers had reached Forges-les–Eaux. Baudouin hang up with a trembling hand. He then advised the President of the War Council. "Can it be our hope is fading? No it can't be! And yet I know that the battle is lost." With the Battle of the Somme won Rommel broke through the British lines and once again caused the defence gap to widen. The French were ordered to form a Paris Army and defend a part of the Seine.

The 51st Highland Division with all its bravery and after a heroic defence surrendered. But Weygand still had not ordered a withdrawal. He was sure the enemy would soon be exhausted. "We are now at the eleventh hour. Hold fast." Not everything was going to the German plan as the 14th Infantry Division of General de Lattre de Tassingly pushed the Germans back taking 800 prisoners. General Guderian reported the on the evening of the 9th June that the French were resisting firmly, and the attack did not proceed beyond a few bridgeheads. Whereas Weygand thought that longer resistance was not possible. He wrote a letter to the President of the War Council stating that the lines may fail at any moment. 'Our armies would fight to the end, but their collapse would be a matter of time.' A counter attack by Buisson's armoured group using their "B" tanks the heaviest in the world that inflicted damage on the lighter panzers. Even when Guderian using a French 47-mm complained the shells were just bouncing off the French tanks. Their overwhelming strength made the French attacks powerful but despite knocking out over 100 German armoured vehicles the B tanks were heavy on fuel which was hard to find at that moment in the Battle, plus their slow speed and lack of mobility were ill adapted to a war of constant movement. On the 10th of June Panzers were seen crossing the lower Seine and the French Government in Paris decided to leave. General Weygand ordered his GHQ to withdraw and as the evening came the news that Italy would enter the war on the German side at midnight, cast the shadow of betrayal. Mussolini spoke to enraptured Italians announced for his balcony high above the Piazza Venezia he had entered the war as a liberator. At Briare, Weygand's HQ on the night of the 11th June, Marshal Petain, Weygand, de Gaulle, Winston Churchill and Anthony Eden met for 3 hours and achieved nothing. The Battle of France was now lost. Yet the battles went on with refugees blocking communications and with some divisions with only a few hundred men.

In one of the towns Cameron and Geordie heard the news of the Italian betrayal and the collapse of Paris on the 14th June. The roads out of Paris were a constant stream of people eventually joining the mobs from Belgium and Northern France. That evening they met a French soldier named Eduard. He was dishevelled and hungry and glad to see them. He was extremely angry to the point of distraction. With head in his hands he told us of arriving at the front and firing a machine gun straight into the German trucks. As the trucks came in he shot the soldiers as they disembarked. "We could have stopped them as they carried out the attacks in the same way. But within a few minutes the soldiers on our flanks ran away. We could have stopped them." He hesitated for a moment and continued. "Some shot themselves in the foot or hand; others broke their arms with heavy rocks. It was not a pretty sight."

There was some like General Pretelat who did not want to retreat but when they did it was far too late. General Weygand had now decided to retreat and mentioned to the War Council for the first time the word armistice. "We should ask the German government for an armistice forthwith." Adding the French can ask for an armistice without blushing. The German Luftwaffe chased the British and French relentlessly bombing the railways and key bridges and roads. Their Panzers and Vehicles used French fuels to drive deep into France. Some of French population had already begun to adjust to occupation and made friendly gestures to the passing invaders. The French S35s tanks gave an excellent account proving to outmatch the German panzers in face to face combat but there were problems with S35s breakdowns and the usual confusion and disorder. Once more a chance was lost on the 17th June.

Marshal Petain broadcast to the French people on the same day. "It is with a sad heart that I tell you we must stop fighting." This inevitably broke much of the French fighting spirit. Mussolini waited till the 20th June before he took the offensive. He had 32 divisions on the Alpine front whereas the French had only 6. But the valleys high in the mountains were narrow and the French artillery lay in wait for them. The observation posts were high above on the summits and could see the Italian deployments. Although the German army had been successful in taking the Alpine Army from the rear there was still fighting in patches. General Conde who had just taken over three French Armies was given the authority to surrender his 400,000 men by General Weygand. On the following day the Italians sealed off France by advancing on Nice. The coastal road was defended by a dozen men on the frontier and held their position to the armistice. At 3.30 pm on June the 21st in the same coach used in 1918 for the armistice the French met Hitler. After reading the Preamble Hitler raised an arm and left the coach. The French were given the text of the meeting that could not be altered. The convention had 24 articles that could not be changed and told they had till 7.30 pm to sign. If not they would be taken back to the outposts. There was no proper discussion of peace terms. When signed the cease fire began at 1.35 am.

Cameron remembered General Weygand saying they only called him in when it was all balled up, 'In three weeks the English will have their necks rung like a chicken.' Maybe he was right but Geordie felt there was not enough effort and communication between the Generals, except sounds of defeat. When Weygand said, "there would be no cowardice in negotiating with the enemy." None other than Marshal Petain agreed and supported him. Weygand admitted to General de Gaulle that after my fight here it won't be a week before Britain was negotiating with the Reich. It was if no one wanted to take actual responsibility for the war. It must have come at an inconvenient time for all of them. But Rommel and the other Panzer Leaders looked from the other side. He had what the opposition lacked and that was faith in victory.

From the trail of events the world and Germany assumed the German HQ was full of military geniuses. Was this so and if there were weaknesses contrary from popular opinion what are they. Robert as a medical man had only a short time to find out as he would certainly be placed in a medical university. In time he was there he heard that Hitler knew his army would never be ready for a war, but neither was the enemy. He had to build his military machine quicker than the rest. The German HQ was far from ready. The scheme for mobilisation did not cover the HQ and therefore not in any way ready. There was no doubt about it the staff were ready. As Hitler travelled in his Fuehrer Special train he left most of the Operational Section behind in the capital. Vivienne wanted this information to be sent as soon as practicable it was to the British advantage and must be exploited. Plus, there was no one to advise Hitler as he was the Leader, Army Commander and Dictator all rolled into one. Such was the confusion at times that when the Red Army moved into Poland Jodl's asked; 'Who Against?' The Army, Navy and Luftwaffe had their own HQs and were not happy that the Wehrmacht Operational Staff were higher than theirs. Vivienne sat on a desk and adjusted her American nylons showing her graceful legs. She noted that the reaction was at first confusion and then curiosity followed by admiration. The room that had been a hive of activity slowed to a halt. It was obvious the staff were not used to seeing such a beautiful woman. Robert felt the same and rushed over to her tugging her off the table. A high ranking officer came over and complimented Vivienne then he asked her if she would like to have some Champaign. Vivienne winked at Robert and strode off with the Officer. Well I don't have the same advantages thought Robert and engaged in asking what he considered interesting questions. Most of the questions the Germans asked were about Vivienne, she had wiped their mind of military matters. Commander Valken appeared and introduced Robert to Gretel one of the highest ranking officers in Germany. He recognised her and laughed. Gretel a small blond with fine features was one of the friends he had when he was last on Germany. He had teased the girls but Gretel he had teased relentlessly. "Yes it's me Robert and you won't pull my leg like you used to. She started to laugh. They walked hand in hand around the room. She explained that Hitler had taken command of the Wehrmacht and had not been interested in organisational problems. There were three commanders in chief that tended to meet only when Hitler was present. The heads of the Oberkommando der Wehrmacht General Keitel thought his duty was to understand Hitler's instructions and convey them to the rest of the staff and was really only a messenger boy. General Jodl a follower of Hitler similar to Keitel but was obsessed with the genius of his leader that had to be followed to the letter. The Operations Staff were split to make them no more than a working staff. Gretel was amused as she continued her explanation. They were basically at loggerheads with each other and had little authority but determined on having a war. During the Polish campaign Hitler decided the new supreme HQ would be located in western Germany as it was now. The Commander in Chief would be Colonel General von Brauchitsch and the new Chief of Staff General Halder. The army staffs were reduced even more. Making the decision to go on the offensive in the west in 1939 was done by Hitler alone on the Fuhrer Special train. He asked no one's advice and discussed it with no one. Until her was sure. Keitel was astounded. Robert was a hungry and suggested a quiet place to eat and talk. "You must have had a difficult time in Britain. Did you not reminisce of the times you were here?" "Yes I did and found tears in my eyes." Robert was telling the truth and remembered watching the events as the Reich grew to become the envy of most of the world. Many distinguished reporters effused on the will and determination of the people of Germany. "But I had to work hard to become a doctor and my speciality of Communicable diseases. Now I would like to find a suitable university to continue my studies." Gretel agreed and told him, she would personally look for a university that suited his talents.

The dinner was good and the French wine rounded off its excellence. Gretel suddenly stood up and gave a Hitler salute, which Robert returned. "I have other duties not as delightful as this, please excuse my leaving. I will contact you soon possible." Robert noted that the men in uniform stood up as soon as Gretel did. He walked around in the rain waiting for Vivienne hoping she would appear soon. The rain stopped and the clouds rolled away brightening up the sky and land. He was home again at least it felt like it. Vivienne arrived all smiles. "Just another conquest I suspect?" Vivienne tickled under his chin. "What do you expect that is what I am here for?" Funny he thought I'm jealous and can't help myself. Would he tell the truth? No its better to wait till the proper time. And when might that be his mind asked. His heart sunk to the bottom of his trousers and refused to reply.

Back with the family at their new found accommodation. They found them sitting by the fire bunched up listening to the German news broadcast. It was always good news rewarded by a military tune blasting the airways. Robert was uncomfortable with Egbert sneaking around the rooms listening to conversations. One morning Robert saw him looking in the keyhole of the bathroom while Vivienne was having her usual bath. He pretended not to see Egbert and kneed him in the side. Egbert yelled and pointed a finger at Robert eye swearing he struck him on purpose. "Sorry my friend but I didn't see you looking in the keyhole." His face turned a bright red as he ran to his mother. Sometimes during a meal Robert imagined kicking Egbert on the shin. But he felt he could be read like a book and put his head down complimenting Erica on her cooking. Vivienne seemed as usual untouched by Egbert's behaviour. One evening Egbert who was always in a hurry to join his Nazi friends ran out the front door with haversack a filled with old cakes and pies that were now turning a shade of green. When Vivienne heard of Egbert's embarrassment at the Nazi event she rushed to his defence. "It could only have been one of his friends playing a boyish trick on him. Better if he puts it behind and gets on with his life." Vivienne sounded so sympathetic that Robert was for a moment fooled. Then he saw her grin break for a second and disappear the next. Egbert friends were clearly unhappy about his prank as he had boasted of his mother's cakes and delights he was expected to bring to the campfire. The guiltier had taken a large bite of a pie and turned a corresponding green, before spitting the mouthful out with tears in his eyes. Egbert's reputation had taken blow and now he was ostracised and was beginning to feel like an outsider. He discovered that being on the outside was hell.

34.

You decide where you go and when to hope.

Five days past before he received a phone message for Gretel, who seemed excited. She told him to meet her outside one of the best restaurants in Berlin. She arrived in a splendid car with a Nazi flag fluttering steadily in the breeze. Gretel dismissed the driver and held out her hand for Robert to take. He did so with some excitement at what she would say. The conversation was light over a rich soup, followed by a fine salad and cold meat. The Brandy was as smooth as it was tasty. Gretel sat back and looked at Robert as if to study him. "I have a great future for you but in the end you must decide." She waited a few seconds for Robert to think of what she was about to say. "In 1937 a SS Medical Academy was founded in Berlin to train active duty medical officers for the Waffen SS and Police. The Building was at first a rented house on Friederichstrasse with only 20 SS officers' candidates. Most of the study was at the University of Berlin. In the autumn of 1940 the Academy was moved to Graz Austria Rosenbergguertel a former state institute for the deaf and dumb. The candidates had to pass out from the SS Junkerschule before they were allowed to join the medial academy. There is a Physical training course and you will spend time in the SS Junkerschule for assault tactics and mobile tactics, these and other subjects will round you off as above average SS Soldier. You Robert will not have to complete all of these but will be allowed to go to the University courses of your Choice. But I advise you to attend Berlin which would be more suitable to you for medical development. And Robert you speak French and English this is ideal in case you have to treat or interrogate them some time in the future. The School Staff Commander is Dr KP Mueller; your main instructor will be Dr Hans Himmler.

The weather over the channel was always difficult to forecast. Goering received a weather warning and cancelled the next attack but too late for two formations of bombers arrived in England without fighter escorts and suffered the consequences. Goering went on to make another intelligence mistake by assuming the north east coast of Britain was not well protected. The idea was to fly from Norway expecting the RAF fighters to be on their way to protect London. This mistake cost Goering twenty four bomber and one fighter with no losses for the RAF. Reports sent by Geordie for the 16th august showed enemy losses greater than ours. Goering had little faith in Radar. The German scientists considered themselves to be the best and their Radar had so far brought little success. They considered their equipment to be far better than the British scoffing at the possibility that it may be in least a little better. German losses from the 8th august to the 26th august were 602 compared to the RAF's 353. Goering not wanting to seem a failure reposted enemy losses of 791. He then changed tactics sending formations of 20-40 bombers protected by around 100 fighters. This strained the RAF allowing the enemy to direct attacks successfully on the RAF fighter airfields. The losses on both sides became near equal. On the British side this created a problem of sufficiency of pilot numbers. The RAF despite its losses had allowed the British Army to build up its numbers and confidence to tackle an invasion force. But Germany had overrun Poland, Norway, Denmark, Holland, Belgium and France. Meanwhile the RAF was still only dropping leaflets, some 6 million! They were not allowed to actually bomb German factories because they were 'private property'!! The Luftwaffe had no such scruples, they'd been developed into an excellent ground attacking force as close support for the Army, fortunately they had not developed any large bombers with defensive armaments they were just so well armed that no plane would stand up to them. But the largest fault was they hadn't reckoned on the RAF, Winston Churchill and the British people.

35.

Hugh Dowding's, Chicks.

On the 10th of May 1940 became Prime Minister and with his speeches slowly changed the mood of Britain. He saw the war as a continuation of the First World War but with new weapons and strategies. He knew Hitler had to defeat Britain but first he had to destroy the RAF. At first the German Luftwaffe began to wear the RAF down and in August there was 103 pilots killed and 128 wounded. They could not train enough new pilots and Dowding's chicks (young pilots) were becoming exhausted. By the end of August, 6 of the 7 sector stations in the south- east group were out of action. But something happened to change the luck of the RAF. Some German bombers accidently dropped their bomb load on London. The RAF in reply bombed Berlin infuriating Hitler. The German bomber raid on the 7th September was huge creating wild panic. Church bells were rung and the Home Guard was called out. So slim were the defences one sector chosen as a landing ground by the Germans the home guard platoon had only one machine gun. Hitler's decision to bomb London gave the RAF a chance to recover. The Luftwaffe expected to sweep the RAF from the skies. But the RAF came to meet them and at one time had all their planes in the air with no reserves. The Luftwaffe turned tail just in time.

Geordie nearly ran over a Polish pilot sitting by the roadside and was amazed to discover he was none other than Aldona Zajac the army officer they had met earlier. He had been inspired when he had heard that Polish airmen were being trained for combat. Still the British high commands were reluctant to send them into battle and extended the flying course to ensure they stayed on the ground. They flew Hawker Hurricanes MK I and on 30th August Ludwik Paszkeiwicz of the 393 squadron ignoring orders not to engage the enemy shot down a German bomber. Aldona was in the Ziemi Pomoroskiej (301 squadron). They and the other squadrons had flown successful missions but again the high ranking officers doubted the number of kills scored. Commander Stanley Vincent flew with the Poles and witnessed their bravery and skills. Soon minds were changed. In the Battle of Britain 32 Polish pilots were lost with 206 Germans killed. Aldona remembered the song 'Till the Lights of London Shine Again' gently playing in his ears as he took off to soar above the cloud base. Aldona had fallen in love with a Scots Girl who had volunteered as an anti-aircraft gunner. She was bright and lovely and Aldona looked on her as a gift from God. Her name was Jenny and suffered from a highland lilt that he found so different from the harsh London accents. There was honesty in her that dominated her personality as well as a good down to earth sense of humour. Aldona would count the hours till he saw her and when they met he hugged her close treasuring these moments. The rest of the time he was so tired he slept soundly except when he woke up trembling in the dark room. One of the pilots had been shot down and his boots had caught in some gear, he spent the few minutes cursing, screaming and praying while the plane spiralled to earth. Aldona dreamt of this death over and over till he appropriated a pair of flying boots near two sizes too big. Other times he dreamt of dancing with Jenny to the tune of 'Till the Lights of London Shine Again.' Amid a mass of uniformed dancers they glided across the floor melting into each other.

36.
The Blitz.

The Blitz followed. The bombing of many cities began on the 7th September 1940 in daylight casualties were 430 killed and 1,600 wounded. Soon the raids became night raids to increase the fear, as Hitler put it to deprive the people of sleep and to weaken them. Tom Redcar was seven when his mother and father were killed in the London bombing while he played in the neighbouring field. He was sent to his aunty Hilda who lived in a flat in the west end. When night bombing commenced he slept with her two boys in a room with a blanket over the window. The bed was comfortable enough but the blasts as the planes approached the area sent us scurrying under the bed. The air raid shelter was at the end of one of the streets and when the alarm was given we stumbled through the streets. The sky opened up in flashes of light and thunderous roars that echoed along the buildings. The firemen ran passed in the direction of the bombing into the danger as if he was late for a bus. Aunty Hilda would say how bloody lucky we are not to be running in his direction. He agreed with her as he was about as scared as it was possible to be. But it is strange how in time it became almost a nightly routine to be expected and endured. Tom was still as scared but he could move when compelled to. He had seen so many others of all ages freeze or back up to a wall and refused to be moved.

The dust caused by a blast or falling buildings haunted the air, coughing and spitting could not be avoided and soon became an inevitable practice. Auntie Hilda's house was still intact except for the line of cracks on the outside walls. The clock that had the pride of place in the living room was stunned into silence at midnight. Its hour hand remained in the twelve positions while the minute hand had fell to six as if it had run out of strength. As the war dragged on scrap metal was in constant demand and wrought iron fences and gates vanished. The Women's Voluntary Services began to extend their help to new situations. The homeless bombed out families were fed in emergency feeding centres and given household utensils. Radio broadcasts sent out signals of comedy and musical shows of all kinds reassuring people that no matter what are happening in the world Britain was still alive and kicking. Many listened to Lord Haw Haw who made people conscious of how ridiculous the Germans and British could be. In Germany the population were not allowed to listen to foreign radio stations a crime punishable by death. In beaten France they were not allowed to listen as in Germany, but as time went by more and more listened to the powerful BBC. Despite jamming by the efficient Germans many of the overrun countries found hope in hearing the bong of BIG Ben and the British national anthem. The BBC continued like a patient Auntie slowly drawing in more of the lost children of the war world. Geordie was watching the building of a coal-hole vault perhaps the least costly type of shelter. It was being built under a pavement with a series of passages for escape. The idea was explained by a construction engineer. The shelters had to be built to disperse the population during the air raids and limiting the distance the public had to walk to a shelter. The crypt of St Martin in the Fields was used for the homeless deep underground and compared with the surface shelters in Grosvenor Gardens. Tom Redcar wondered if the surface shelter as a public toilet. "Hay mister." he asked Geordie. "Is it ok to have a pee in there?" "I doubt, it but you can use the back of it if you are desperate." Tom came back and started to ask lots of questions. "Watch out there may be chatter bugs around." Warned Geordie while trying his best to look serious and waving a finger. "Tittle-tattle can cost lives and cause disaffection." Tom desperately not wanting to be called a tittle-tattler murderer whatever that was. "I didn't mean to cause disinfection." Tom ran like a hare when he saw some his friends across the road. Geordie had heard the news of the attempted assassination of Hitler in Munich

Burgerbraukeller. Hitler had been in a hurry although it was the sixteenth anniversary of the failed Putsch in 1923. He wanted to get back to Berlin as soon as possible and had just left the building fifteen minutes before. The blame lay with the British Intelligence Service and rewards of £45,000 were offered. Would everyone have just gone home and the war called off if it had been successful? Would the heads of the states have a party to celebrate the end of a lunatic? Would Russia give up the lands it had invaded in Poland? With the war gone and the countries at peace would it influence Japan to leave China? And would it end the food shortage. During the weekends in France which was beginning already to feel the pinch, the people took their bicycles and by went by train to the countryside to search out extra food. Now the same was being done in an unexpected result of Hitler's German victories.

As the Blitz went on the framework of the great city of London was interrupted and many places destroyed. The roads, rail links, industry and the dockyards were targeted. The anti-aircraft gunners were targets of large high explosive bombs most of them were Royal Marines in their teens. He heard the young voices shouting orders amid the noises of hell as Geordies knees felt weak and could not stop tears coming to eyes at this shear impossible scene. Through it all Geordie could not help but admire the resilience of the ordinary people. He watched each night when one or two hundred bombers came over the majority of Londoners stayed at home. He wondered at their thoughts as each night passed and in the morning trooping of to work. Much had to be repaired quickly to keep the wheels of industry turning. The days and nights moved into one like a long symphony with its drama and sweet tones with loud crashes from the drum section and then pauses then beginning again. By the Month of November 1940 other cities were picked as targets such as Liverpool, Southampton, Coventry, Glasgow and Plymouth. He thought of the boy and girl sent to Plymouth and began to shoulder some of the blame for them being in city the Germans would certainly have targeted in time. At times his hands began to shake but when he heard the women joke as they moved amongst the rubble as if it were an ordinary day. He watched with wonder as the female volunteers and fire fighters cheerily walked to work. In each city along with people being targeted and infrastructure, books by the million were destroyed many irreplaceable, dropping society toward barbarism.

Time did seem to stop for moments and then race to fill an alien year that would be remembered as long as life. Thankfully the raids on London became less frequent and some normality crept into the fabric of the city life. London the largest open target in the world had won and Geordie celebrated with his friends in the news business. But the raids although less frequent were still deadly. A German fighter air craft would fly out of the blue and strafe people walking down a street. Sometimes it would be a woman pushing a pram and at other times people enjoying a walk in a park. War was never like this nor was it professed to be by the military geniuses or arm chair warrior. Geordie thought he could do more than just file a story of people struggling along in war conditions. So in a moment of patriotic fervour and boredom he volunteered for something more dangerous.

37.

There are no Secrets to Success.

In November 1940 the SOE (Special Operations Executive) was formed and Geordie for his sins was sent to one of the new schools as a potential agent. He found himself unbelievably natural at deception and a sponge at the intake of information. After all of his adventures physically tough and had a good supply of endurance, agile and strong. In fact he had the makings of a SOE Operative. Quite willing to train all night in all weathers and then run for miles along a pebbled beach. Geordie was as keen a trainee operative as the new service had seen. They asked him on completion of train if he was interested in becoming an instructor, but he was unwilling to play games rather than do the real thing. He was glad to be assigned to active service and say goodbye to bed sheets and fancy knives and forks. Of the many pubs and bars, where the scraping noises of moved tables and chairs and talk was as worthless as the smoke that filled them. His enthusiasm was rewards in a prompt mission in the art of resistance.

Geordie was sent to invigorate resistance in the lowlands and France. But with the lack of arms he was forced to circulate clandestine leaflets. This was extremely dangerous as the German could easily trace back along the hand-out line. The German police exacted a heavy toll. Strangely most of the resistance was recruited after listening to the BBC which sent messages and directives. Most of all it sent out messages of hope. Even French soldiers left over from Dunkirk were helped to evade captivity.

Geordie had a narrow escape the following day after he had arrived. He knew he was being watched but felt safe as he knew the person well, how unusual to meet someone from your home town in such a short time arriving in an occupied territory. He even waved and smiled at the man as anyone would have done, this friendly gesture was returned and Geordie felt he was in safe hand and sure the man would keep our little secret. However as the man moved away and two men in Geordies' group came running silently but showing signs of concern. When they reached Geordie one of the men his voice shaking told Geordie that the man he waved at was a well-known informer and would be sending information on what he saw to the nearest Gestapo office. Geordie swore and threw his leaflets down and stamped on them wishing he had never come in the first place. They ran left at the next turn hoping they would not bump into the local Gestapo group. One man pointed ahead and the other pointed to the right. Nothing was said they just kept running with as much energy they could expend. Geordie after some time arrived at abandoned stables a mile out of the town. He ran into the place which had been deserted for year or two and climbed a fragile ladder to the dark recess where he had slept nights and lay worrying until well into the early hours. He looked for his hiding place and found his credentials this was just in case he had to leave France. He had to make his way back to the HQ underground base but it was too travel at this time as workmen were finishing work and would be scrutinised by the Germans in detail. Geordie became frustrated and decided to make a move slowly as the light began to fade quickly. He had prepared himself for the meeting at their Headquarters. His clothes were already begun to look dishevelled and dirty. There was nothing to do but brush himself with a bush branch. He walked slowly down the empty side road towards the main pathway. It would be safer as many Germans patrolled the river routes into town and this pathway was for lovers in the evening including Germans. It was cold and he lifted his collar to heat his neck against a stiff breeze that was building up. The mist was drifting from the river and noises of the currents sounded like whispering. At the edge of the town people with carts were going towards the late market. They had vegetables for a German targeted market and making a tidy little sum of money, which caused some resentment in the less fortunate in town. Food

136

was always spare but you could always find a potato if you searched hard enough. No one waved or spoke everyone just stayed within their own groups and walked.

Geordie put his hands in his pocket to warm up a little. He thought this casual gesture would be good just now. He was not far from Headquarters when he saw within the mist which was clearing a group of ten Germans and they were in a hurry. He kept his head up as they rushed past him. He held his breath and listened for any information. One German shouted "Sie verstecken sich heraus nahe Herr Klinsman's Bauernhof. Schnell mussen wir keine Zeit verlieron." 'Oh God,' he thinks to himself, they think we are staying at one of the farms. It's a good idea to move out further from the path centre. He then puts his fist sharply onto his lips to stop him shouting out insults to the running Germans. They rush by him as if he were not there; he was as far as they were concerned invisible. He quickens his pace but is careful to look as if not too much in a hurry. At last he arrives to find the headquarters empty. He felt great anxiety for the others, where were they now? He washed his face and looks in the mirror. He felt 10 years older in that one day. Where could they have gone? I might go and look for them, he thought, but he decides to wait in case they had taken a longer route. Half an hour passed and there was no sign of anyone and did not know what to do next. He felt a new kind of fear and began to shake a little. When he heard a familiar voice whispering his heart slowed so he could feel the loss of pressure. Standing up he saw Mark. "Thank god you are safe but where is Robert." The answer was as he expected. "He ran to one of the farmsteads in the south probably one of his relations

During the late afternoon a leader of the resistance appeared and gave orders for a quick action to be taken against a Gestapo and Army patrol that would be sent to ambush incoming planes on a well-known landing site. It was on a flat piece of ground on an elevated row of hills idea cover from the land and air. Geordie and Mark included made up a unit of thirty. This made them at least ninety less that the Germans. But surprise would be on their side. It seemed as usual the weather turned to wild wind and rainy. The dark added to their hiding ability but it was also counterproductive in that the enemy were party invisible. Especially, on the roads that were channelled thought the forests. The hills were drenched and muddy with large clumps of grass islands surrounded by slippery slime.

They waited at the edge of the forest where the Germans had plans to split and cover the high and low sides of the landing site. This was done with the usual German efficiency and two groups vanished into the wall of rain. Geordie slipped on a mud embankment and buried half his face in the slime ground and cursed in French, British and German. He rolled over on his side and cuddled his SMG with the barrel near his lips. An order was given and they moved off towards the high part of the hill. It took some time stopping to find their direction as the rain was trying to prove how much it could fall like a single sheet in the least time. At a muddy corner after some discussion the lead men moved gingerly along. Mark was the point man and he had his mind on the route ahead and the next familiar point, which was a lone tree that leaned over the embankment. A German SS soldier appeared in an instant right in front of Mark. He hesitated wondering for that second if this was real. His training took over and the blast of this SMG filled the night air. The SS man fell forward and struck Mark heavily as his steel helmet fell on his knees. Mark did not wait for another appearance and fired into the dark. Screams came lowed and frequent and the nine millimetre round beat a small group on the German patrol. The partisans rushed forward to be met by a determined group of SS. Geordie had trained for this but he was surprised at the ferociousness of the enemy and life and death struggle in the night. The SS man was young and strong gripping like steel battering his head into Geordie's face knocking a tooth out and thickening his upper lip. Geordie quickly lowered his head and caught the SS man butting forwards, knocking him out. Georgie pulled out his knife and plunged it into the enemy's throat. The rain ran down the Germans face taking with it the blood from his throat and over Geordies knife hand. A butt of a rifle struck Geordie on his head and caused him to fall into the dark. He was isolated and lost for that time pointing his weapon in as many directions as he could. Two SS man came rushing with bayonets directed at him. He knew he was a goner and as his SMG clicked empty. He fumbled for another magazine which was wet and muddy that spun in the air from his slimy hand. He tried to grab it but it seemed to spin from right to left. He drew out a grenade and stood his ground as the pin flew in the mid-air. He held the lever tight in front of himself facing the base plate at the enemy. The Germans bumped into each other and froze. They knew that at that distance they would be struck by hot shrapnel and one unluckily be hit by the base plate. Their minds were made up swiftly and they vanished into the night taking their fear with them. Geordie knew this was not over with and resolved to do the best he could in the fight. The sound of light tanks filled the wild weather air and the SS leaped over the sides of the Lorries. They knew exactly what they were doing and spread out to form firing lines. The two women who had shown bravery over the last few months were quick to appreciate the danger. Both were called Rebecca and known to the group as Beth1 and Beth2. Their leather jackets gleamed in the rising moonlight and rain and blast of their SMGs and the heavy thud of grenades blasting the muddy ground. Scream and brave shouts mingled as the groups of six began to be cut down by the Spandau machine guns. One of the Beth's spun and fell making Geordie determined to at least do some damage to the SS. In dark his group of six made a quick move to the flank of the Germans and fired the only two French machine guns, they fired low and cut the legs of those standing. Some of the SS took cover under the Lorries as their light tanks searched the area with sprays of machine gun fire. Another six of the partisan group were on higher ground and began to throw grenades on the roof of the tanks. As quick as possible the partisan group vanished leaving behind the German professionals confused. The dark and the rain with a passive moon gave them cover to run after blasts from every weapon they had. For that second they held the fire fight and the advantage was that few minutes for a getaway. Racing over the hill to the parked vehicles two miles away they were silent with the exception of gasps of breath. Geordie was filled with a silent deep sadness for those braves he had left behind dead and those unfortunately wounded. They would suffer the hell of captivity and torture in damp dirty cells interrupted by accomplished torturers. Reth1 urged those who fell behind to catch up displaying considerable stamina. Scrambling into the vehicles they shouted for the drivers to drive on at top speed. Soon they were back near the edge of the town and were dropped off in twos. The SS and Gestapo as usual had side streets cut off with sandbags and machineguns. Only one was held for questioning. It was young Raymond just turned eighteen. He knew the cost of capture not only to him but to all of his relations. He slipped two grenades into hands slipping the prepared pins out and shouted out in Russian. The blasts killed two of the SS and made Raymond unrecognisable. His cry in Russian removed any chance of recognition locally.

The next morning was one a greater tension as they all knew that retributions would take place first by going to the mayor's office and demanding a list from which they would take at least one hundred names. Or the Germans would walk the streets pick people at random. Sometimes they would bang on doors and wait for the unsuspecting dweller to answer. Old men women and children were not exempt in fact Geordie noticed a kind of pleasure they took of picking the elderly and the youngest as a show piece of their powers. The town square or a convenient wall near a church the innocent town people would be lined up. The rain had relented and the sun was about to show its power when the retribution – were marched to the centre of the town, some were talking, chattering while others begged to be set free. Other would beg for their relations to be let off to work the farm for the remnants of their family.

The old man Geordie saw with his binoculars had the leftovers of the famous regiment for the shirt. Beside him were two six year old boys imitating his every move? Geordie could not hear any speech which he was thankful for. They lined up in two rows. The first fifty including the old man and children were first against the wall. The children clanked at the old man a stood to attention. The machine guns cut them down within seconds before anyone could think of an argument to stay alive while others would die. The next group were mostly young women and it seemed their elderly parent. Who could tell except they held hands tightly knowing what they had seen was about to happen to them for not reason they could tell of. An elderly women and a young man ran out and grasped the rifles of the military firing shad that backed up the machine gunners. On weapon that was turned shot a German officer in the stomach, he creased and moaned wriggling on the wet ground. A woman ran forward to help him but was shot by an officer with his pistol. She looked shocked that this would happen even to those who wanted to help. Geordie quick as he could chose seven of the best shots and ordered them to find a target and shot for all they were worth. The effect at near seven hundred yard away was that of shear panic and bewilderment that anyone would dare to shot at them. The town's people ran in all directions making it impossible to shoot in case they hit one of their own. Meanwhile a scream and arms thrown in the air as the bullets struck part of their body. The main machine gunner was hit in the knee and his knee cap splintered in red. Some shots were fired from near windows killing members of the firing squad. A series of grenades rolled on the ground to find a German surprised as they shattered their arms and bodies. The surviving officers swore revenge before he was cut down by a bullet in the throat but still driven by hate ran on all fours along the street. His gage became slower and slower until he became statuesque. His buttocks thrust upwards and his face in a muddy puddle.

For the remainder if the day there was a complete blanket silence over the town as many of the population were slowly vanishing to the winds. When German reinforcements arrived the town had changed but the retributions were carried out with greater severity. Geordie wondered if his actions had caused more trouble and heartache that necessary. His only gain he knew was some of the people had helped in the revenge act. Nonetheless the town was drowned in salience.

38.
The Return.

He never thought we would be sent back to the same area of France after causing so much trouble to the Germans and the killings of the people in the village. But the thought of a bloody informer lounging there is enough to make him change his attitude. "Have we any idea who it might be, it could be Robert?" The British Officer rubber his jaw and fixed his clear green eyes on Beth. It was as if he waited for her to give him an indication that the risk would be worth it. "Clearly, I have a mission to make the plans for the day we have to assist an allied invasion but they may all come to nothing if we are caught short by a spy. The plans may become unravelled and if they do, even by Robert our good friend, we intend to rescue, then heaven help him and the rest of us. From the premise we have to search out this bastard whoever they are and put paid to his life and plans. The price may be high but that is what we do and are fed and trained for. "Do you all agree?" The group as one shouted "Down with traitors." The meant the sentiment as they now thought they could see the end some year or so away.

I thought that was where you were going. I haven't seen him since then." Geordie then tells Mark what they heard the Germans say on the way here. The Gestapo and the others think we are all together. That bloody informer had not waited long enough to watch us leave probably thought we would stay together in one bunch. That's a bit of luck but we need to see if Robert is alright." "Yes come to my place we need to eat to keep us going also it's not far from here. Let's have something warm to eat and then see what we can do. I need something I'm cold fragile and starving and I have a need to clean up." They left together and within a few minutes arrive at Mark's home. The morning sun came up pushing through a bank of grey cloud and spun a light web over the town river. There was a silence different from early mornings for there was no one there to break it. There were no church bells, no market construction nor children at play. No one was alive to greet the day.

Geordie and the others swiftly ran for the hills and made contact with the others named Marquis after the scrub on the south west hills. They continued their education on how to destroy the German transport and communication lines. Help teaching all the factions of partisans to work together to kill a professional enemy that was hated throughout Europe and to take advantage of any enemy weaknesses to bring their capabilities to a sudden end. And fear in the night. They did not look heroic or even effective, just ordinary. The all had nick names to hide their identity not just for their own being but to protect their families and friends. Beth 2 sat impatiently puffing at a cigarette then lighting another. Geordie wanted to reduce his intake of cigarette smoke and now only took a ciggy in the evening. "Beth I want you to come with me on this show. I need a good man." Beth smiled and tossed her lovely black hair over her right shoulder exposing a china white neck. Geordie wandered if the rest of her was as smooth and white. One thing was certain she hatred the Bosch. The Bosch as she called them had destroyed her life without so much as a pig would thank you for a waste meal. She in return could be relied to kill them without so much as waiting for a thank you. Her cold bloodiness was ideal for war time but he knew that women like her could change and fit in any domestic situation in short time. She would make a good wife to someone who did not ask too many questions.

The group of partisans welcomed the next fight and the exposure of a traitor in the village. The village was called Rosa a back water of isolated France where after the war Geordie would love to retire to in contentment. The breeze was light at the beginning of the evening and the clouds were long and grey. The sky complimented the lush green of the farm lands with a light blue and a dull sun of orange.

The river swayed along the shortened grass and reeds tumbling over the shale and chalk changing colour and speed at intervals. The birds were high in the air some circling and dropping to a spot of advantage. An upset blackbird burst out of a hedge exploding green leaves that randomly landed on the rocks that had formed a bundle in a sea of green. The little village was now near and Beth 2 signalled to change to the working cloths similar to the local garb. The left the other cloths abandoned under a heavily branched tree situated close to the meandering river. They arrived at a small cottage on the outskirts of the village. It had small windows and rusted implements of various kinds leaning against the peeling white paint of the cottage. Not wishing to warn the occupants they went through the door quickly. A woman stood up and shouted for her husband in the next room. Both shivered despite the bright fire. "We are looking for someone you may know who knows a lot about the daily habits of the village. You may have seen them talking to the police or someone in authority." Geordie felt he had covered everyone in the village but he had to get them thinking. A fire flickered warmly and an iron pot of stew bubbled away unconcerned of the words and action in the cottage. The woman threw herself into the arms of her husband; her eyes flashing in fear. Her husband looked around at the antagonists hoping to see a friendly face. There was none. "I know you are looking for the informer but he is not known to us. He is a man or woman of the shadows. It would be certain death for me and my family if I became involved in such actions." The fire flickered and cat ran to the base of a cupboard and sprung with amazing agility right to the top, before settling down as if to witness the happenings below. There was a knocking on the door of rapid successive urgency. It had to be someone or something of importance to be banging on a door during a curfew. They all froze except Beth. Beth was instantly at the door and opened it sharply. She had expected to find an enemy that would have died instantly by her hand. It was Robert gasping for breath and ragged. "They have you in the village and will be here shortly." Robert gasped out as he hung on to the door. "Let's go." Robert demanded. They ran out into the slow progressive light of the morning and left behind two people glad that they and survived another dangerous moment in war. The small pavements and muddy roads ran into the darkness of alleyways and then into the light of squares. The Gestapo and their French compatriots were now everywhere and soon spotted the group of partisans. Machinegun fire filled the air with ricochet's and loud thumps, noisy panicky voices with scuffles amid the roar of motor vehicles. "It's down here." Robert shouted pointing to the narrow passageway between two large cottages. There was a narrow pipeline that ran to the open ground near the river leading to the hills. Robert grabbed Geordies jacket shoulder and led him with force to the pipeline. The others followed with the exception of two men intent on capturing the traitor at any expense. A heavy machine gun opened up and scattered pieces of brick and metal into the dim light. Geordie was hit in the thumb and blood pumped skywards. Robert quick of the mark impressed a British bandage over the wound and tied it tight. Robert at this point was lifting his wounded partner and made ready to run when a burst of bullets beat over his back. Robert was dead before he fell on Geordie. In the final darkness of the pipeline the remains of the party moved with all the power a human being could convey to worn and injured body. The party threw themselves into the river. The last man in was shot in the spine as he jumped as far as he could and hoped to the safety of the river. He laid face up whispering; his eyes fixed to the last stars in a confused sky of flashes and racing smoke. Beth touched his face and whispered in his ear as she let him go to be carried in the current. The wounded man picked up speed and his body whirled spinning clockwise down to a weir. The hills were now a mass of rain and each slope was treacherous allowing gravity to take advantage. Their bodies tired beyond all the training they had been given carried on as automats. There were passed moaning even the British officer was quiet. Geordie tried to keep his thump up to prevent it becoming affected by the mud. But that became impossible and soon he plunged that hand deep in to find a lever to propel him upwards. Far in the hills the weather was cold and the ground was brittle and frosty, many bodies were grouped in families and single travellers frozen and still. They were quiet and motionless uncaring of the winds and snow. Geordie made sure he was not going to became one of them and switched up another gear set his mind and body to win. Back in a safe area of the Marque Geordie's mind settled to almost normal

The woman and the man they had met in the first cottage came into the camp followed by a boy in his teens. After a long talk with the leaders they informed the rest the boy was the traitor. He was the son of the local policemen who had come originally for London. Beth stepped forwards and volunteered to shot him. Geordie asked if he could go along as he wondered if Beth would actually shoot. He remembered the kindness to the man in the river and this was one of the things that casted a doubt on her capabilities.

The place she chose was a tree that leaned over to a loose ground of sand. She asked the youth to stand next to the sand. He looked at her carefully and smiled. He had an idea she liked him and his youthful looks and he would lessen her will and set him free. Beth turned her back to him and spun back slowly. Her pistol pointed at the boy's chest. He screamed. Beth's pistol fired four times and her smile grew at each shot. Her heart was empty.

39.

Back to dear old Blighty.

"What now?" Geordie asked pleased to be back in Blighty, but had the feeling he was needed elsewhere. "Do I go back to France or some other place?" "Okay have lunch at HQ then we shall meet soon as time is important in this next mission. Are you happy with that?" Geordie was given a watermarked note which ordered him to France, as he expected. But he had to admit not so soon. He was amazed; he thought it would be days before another job would be given to him as the British tended to take their time even in war. He almost mentally tripped at the thought, as he had intended to telephone his old friends and maybe unite for an afternoon in the old haunts. In fact he secretly thought a little rest would be good and thought his will to get into another operation was over silly enthusiasm in this dangerous game.

The men in uniform in an elaborated silver framed picture on the fire mantle, showed war does not give you too many holidays anyway and not too much picture taking. He got up and went to the dining hall he felt hungry for some wholesome home cooking. A good feed did help as he had not eaten well in France but what amazed him was his thirst which was nearly insatiable. In the past he would have dived for the bar and stayed till told to go home. Now he more interested in cool British water soft and clean. Maybe he wanted to keep his wits about him and he could not think of better advice he hoped would contribute towards his longevity. At lunch he enquired if anyone had seen Cameron, Molina, Larry or Robert. He talked to three officers who were more than attentive that knew them quite well. Cameron and Molina had been seen visiting several places and were apparently quite romantic at times and most guessed they were on the way to have a wartime romance. The officers were mostly in agreement of the same thoughts of their wife's and families, they were constantly on their minds. The separation from their loved ones was amplified by the dread of German bombing of the British cities. The bombs dropped had no soul, bereft of feelings of sympathy may even now have taken their beloveds without them knowing. This was a constant worry.

Larry he knew was overseas on a capital ship and hopefully be returning home soon, but rumours had it that the Navy was in a flux with the submarine problem. No one mentioned Robert perhaps they did this on purpose or out of politeness. Geordie sank into the comfortable chair and slipped from the conversation and fell into a silence, before he drifted into memories of the war. The war of memories he suspected would last much longer than any tangible war. It had artfully invaded his mind and unexpectedly met his faculties of thoughts on the road of life, met as a stranger and then accompanied him thereafter for the duration of his existence. The memory did so without his permission. It was to him an inconsiderate companion stealing a ride on his very being.

It wasn't long before someone switched on ITMA the radio show that was so popular it was a vital to the lives of millions. They made a game of picking their favourite characters in the auditory entertainment. Some preferred Sydney Keith or Horace Percival or one of the ladies such as the wonderful Dorothy Summers. They laughed at the jokes some of which were quite risqué but in this time of war the jokes became acceptable and became a component of British humour. He enjoyed the lunch chatting and laughing at some of the remarks made by the others who seemed to have invented a new prospective of absurdity he suspected due to the fondness of the ITMA show. He felt good and ready for a welcome cup of tea that would salve and heal his soul. It may be just what the doctor ordered. As the evening progressed some of the company left with only a few remaining. Geordie waved as they went past him on the way to the darkening streets. He thanked them for their company and genuinely meant the sentiment. He never felt so good in a long time; it was strange being an introvert he was now in a peculiar need of company. Or was he just dammed lonely and needed his fellow man around him as the nearness of danger had enhanced and opened his heart to the want of company.

A young gentleman without uniform arrived at the door of his room and announced that tea and coffee would be served in the Commanders office. They all got up and walked slowly looking happy and as they came into the room each made a dash for a comfortable chair. The attendant asked Geordie what he wanted to drink as he sat down. "Tea would be ideal, thank you." "Can we smoke in here? I'm giving up after this packet is finished so I'm just going to enjoy what I have left." "Good for you." said the Commanding Officer as he settled in the comfort of the large chair. "Let's talk now." He leant forward and looked around him there were twelve men in the room and all of them alert to his words. "We are looking for a man who has worked with us for a long time and unfortunately he has stopped contacting us. He is in Berlin and we want to get him back home. He may be dead in prison or has even changed allegiance. If not, he will have enough knowledge by now of the German power and weakness. If we can get him out, then who knows we could end this war sooner than later. We need someone who he would trust, someone he knows and someone brave enough to want to get him out of Germany."

Geordie doesn't listen anymore and interrupts the speaker." Well if it's someone who he can trust, how you can afford to pick me. I've probably never met the man it just doesn't make sense." The man sitting beside Geordie decides to talk and does not let Geordie finish. "It's Robert we want home." "Robert! Robert who how! You don't mean my friend Robert, but he is not in Germany I thought he was still in France. I asked around when I was there I had people looking for him. Well I never, Good old Robert what a brave man. No wonder no one mentioned his name at lunch. Am I still the right choice Cameron or even Larry would be better people." "No we want you because you were the one who was closest to Robert as far as we know. Your skills are good and you speak fluent French and German." Geordie stands up and takes a cigarette from his packet and lights it while everyone is just sitting in silence looking to him. "I hope you have a good plan as one small mistake could kill us both. Even in France I felt when in danger I would somehow get out, but in Berlin itself there are few ways to get back safely." The commanding officer stood up facing Geordie and spoke; we will try to make a plan that is right for you and as safe as we can make it." Geordie almost stood on the officer's foot as he stepped forwards to shake his hand. "Until tomorrow we will meet and discuss everything, and pick your identity." He was now wondering what he had to do in Berlin."

Geordie was never one of those certain people that sailed through life in an open boat. His was more one of many faults and stormy seas. In this very room he felt alive and fearful but ready to do what was required of him. Should he be able to find Robert there was still the problem of how he will escape. "It's an open plan to give you as much scope as you need. There will be others with you and they will help. Get some rest and we will talk tomorrow morning." They all rise out of the chairs and shake Geordie's hands before departing. Geordie goes to his isolated quiet room and sits on the bed thinking. What have I done? I got carried away. How do I tell them tomorrow if I've changed my mind? He begins to sweat badly as if fear had clung to him tightly around the neck. He wipes away the sweat but more comes until his collar is soaking. He takes off his jacket to finds his shirt heavy and very damp. He is scared and not sure if he can do this thing he had promised to do. He goes over to the sideboard slightly unsteady and pours himself a drink of whisky, he starts to shake badly and doesn't bother with water which he would normally add and drinks all of the glass down. What am I going to do? I'm a coward I'd give Robert away if I reacted like this. They will need to find someone else a much braver man. He lies on the bed and his head begins to swirl and he falls into a deep sleep that takes him to the following morning. Geordie was awakened with a fright. He had been dreaming of the old days when as a boy he had fallen into the river and thankfully Robert had saved him. I do owe Robert my life and surely that is worth an effort to save him. He thinks to himself remembering Roberts's brave encounters since the war began.

Geordie then considers that maybe I can do this. Now Robert knew he would always look after his friends as it was definitely the proper thing to do and this was an opportunity to prove it. I will speak to the men downstairs about my doubts, I've got to be truthful no use going to help if I'm a coward.

He dresses and makes his way to breakfast. He nods to others on the way downstairs but does not speak. Most of the men have already arrived and when the Commander sees him he stands up from his seat. "Good morning Geordie did you not have time to shave did you sleep in." Geordie feels the stubble on his chin and replies "Yes I did in fact." "You must be hungry then let's start with a good English breakfast." "Yes great idea I'm quite hungry." Nothing much was said at the table and when they had finished eating Geordie stood up and said he would shave before their meeting and be ready in an hour. They all nod in agreement and make their way to their chosen destinations. Geordie shaves and cleans himself up and does so without thought of the oncoming day. He makes his way to the meeting room and sees that everyone had arrived. The Commander uses a hand gesture to show Geordie his seat next to him. Geordie sits down and right away starts to tell them all about last night. He stands up and almost shouts. "Do you think I can do this?" No one makes a comment but most put their faces down towards the floor. Stephen who knows Geordie gets up and moves towards him and puts his hands on his shoulders. "Look Geordie we are all scared I'm off to get involved again at the front. You know yourself that the adrenalin you feel is about survival and you don't cram up. Some do, but with your experience you can play the part. I'm sure you can. The Commander then speaks "Look if you go you would be well prepared. You won't be directly in German HQ as Robert was our number one Agent. Our number two has been trying to trace him but needs help. Your job at near HQ would be that as an ordinary man working serving food to the men and listening to conversations for any word of Robert. It's difficult and dangerous but please give it some thought." Geordie smiles for the first time that morning as he thought that he would be a high ranking Nazi and did not like the idea, but this one suited him. He can speak German and best of all he knew many jokes.

He knew number two agent in Germany. "I'll go." He said confidently. "Let's get stated on the briefing," They each salute him and one by one as they make their way into another room some patted Geordie in the back.

40.

The Lysander Trips.

The Lysander lay in the shadow of a lone tree that even the full power of the full moon could not penetrate. Its engine started and the night air became full of a feeling of action. The SOE were lending a hand in the spreading of organized resistance and could not bear to miss this crazy enterprise. Geordie was glad to have company on this and of the operation, two of the company were American and as keen as it was possible to be. Mat was from New York and had a New Jersey accent as well as being a Golden Glove boxer. The night he met him there was a vicious fight in the local public house that seemed impossible to stop. It was a Merchant Seaman as tough as old boots who took exception to an ex policemen calling him names. The sailor did not even get up from his seat and leaned to place a right hook on the policemen jaw which dropped him like a rag doll. The bar erupted into a melee where everyone wanted to show their prowess in belligerence. The merchantman held his ground against the local lads and knocked out four men in quick succession. This stopped the fight for a minute as they began to gang up on him. This seemed so unfair to Mat, he walked into the gang of locals and in a flurry of punches dropped two and injured another. The Merchant Seaman joined in and soon there was no one to fight. Instead of shaking hands with Mat the sailor swung a punch at his. It clipped Mats ear as bobbed to avoid the blow. Mat struck with a stunning right that rocked his adversary but he did not fall. He shook his head and came on again as Mat moved back a little to avoid the rain of blows. Some on both sides thudded with sickening power. The final blow came from Mat as threw as series of combination punches pushing the sailor backwards to the side of the bar. Trapped there he became wild and punched in the air swearing he would kill. An upper cut so perfect in its design and effort hit the sailors jaw nerve sending him in spin. He hit the floor with a resounding thud and lay quiet. The barman shouted for an on the house round of drinks that was greeted with a cheer that was usually saved for the queen. The night was improved by the sailor who came too and congratulated Mat on his skill as a fighter. Austin was a Texan that had the slowest drawl and most casual attitude Geordie had encountered. It was easy to like Austin as he didn't have an ounce of meanness in his body. He would ramble on about the wide Texas sky and his golden haired girl back home that was intended to make the others jealous. This worked and the other two would listen with a mountain of envy at these well spun stories.

During a previous conversation he learned some of the details that were not exactly secret which he found interesting. He rethought of the SOE and British Intelligence and the rest of Europe. The page of resistance turned against the Germans when they invaded Russia. The Communists blamed the Capitalists for all of the troubles in the world. Now there is a new chapter where all resistance groups no matter what political stance. It seems all sins and combined to face a mutual enemy. The Germans by blaming the communists was the best incentive call to action. They were now a unified action advised by Moscow or secret courier. The more success the soviets had the greater the resistance. While in Poland, Greece, Rumania and Yugoslavia the two resistance factors squabbled and clashed. But the important aspect of this operation is flying over France aiming to the south and then to the north later. The dropping off point for the Americans is to increase the resistance and bring some kind of cohesion to this stage of the war. The slow grouping was due to the Communist not joining forces for a concerted action against a strong German existence in France that is now seen to be growing. Geordies American friends have help them put their individual aims behind and work closer. There was also the training and arming and the gathering of information as in the others occupied nations. This did not seem to matter at the moment as they boarded the Lysander engine and blade spun into action awakening the night sounds. Geordie wasn't sure which SOE liaison airlift it was he guessed it was No161 Special Duties flight from Newmarket and dropping them off into the arms of their SOE Agents called, Joes. At level fight and over the channel the Lysander often called the Scarlet Pimpernels of the sky tried out the two fixed browning .303 machine guns and the .303 Lewis gun in the rear cockpit. The flash and the chatter of the guns made the men in the plane feel an element of confidence while in the pitch dark over the solemn grey waters. Their equipment was in the parachute supply canisters under their feet and was of great importance to the mission. Part of Mats job during that part of the mission was to report the supply of weapons that the resistance was crying out for. Austin was an expert in document forgery just as vital as guns. He was also the radio operator knowing that not keeping up with the changes in the Nazi Bureaucracy would be a fatal to the groups. Both man had a choice of weapons that was settled in the matter of Sten guns a favorite of the Copenhagen group. The wind was wild tossing the plan around making the occupants sway despite being strapped in. They were mostly silent and buried in their thoughts. Mat was a pipe smoker and had his pipe fixed firmly in his tight lips but sometimes let it point upward and settle back to its firm position. Geordie wondered what was in his mind in relation with the movements of the pipe; he was tempted to ask for pennies worth of Mats thoughts as the rain battered on the fuselage drumming up a sense of awareness of them being high in the air and under thick clouds. The hours passed and a sense of tension dropped to a mild relaxation allowing them more free movement and shot to each other over the engine drone. The pilot relayed to them they were in the southern region of France and would be seeing lights of a city far below. This stirred the interest of the men who were now looking for some diversion.

Out of the sky approaching the front of the Lysander a Me109 night fighter appeared under a wide moon. It was an appearance that startled the heart of the pilot to burst into a thumping action. Their machineguns fired wildly towards the moon as the German fighter swung expertly to their left and lined up to fire in three bursts. The pilot was wounded in the face and shoulder but kept control of the plane pointing the joystick down towards what light was visible from the city far below. The others sat immobile with fear on hearing gunfire. Bullets whipped in front of them ricocheting randomly. One stray hit Austin square in the chest causing his blood to shoot out and splatter Geordie. Austin's face was that of unbelievable surprise and then to a quiet paling resignation. His head fell to one side. All of this happened with a second or two. The Lewis gun fired a long hopeful burst and then died in the new silence as the engine stuttered and failed. The plane stalled and dropped whistling the wind like a cry for help. There was not thing Tex and Geordie could do but sit and hope. The moments were now in that slow motion where time was not entirely suspended but halted to a snail's pace. The plane lifted slightly as it tore into long grass and skipped over mud and lost a wing on the wide tree. It spun to the left and to the right before its nose dipped into a stream. The body of the plane lifted and stayed at thirty degrees making Mat and Geordie fall towards the cockpit when they released their straps. They crumpled by the pilot who as still quite conscious and in a foul mood. He ranted and raved about their bad luck and promised a better trip the next time. Then he died as blood filled his mouth and overflowed on to the deck. This was the moment to move and get whatever supply that was undamaged. They looked around and realised they were the only survivors but this was only for a quantum moment as they knew their very lives were in immediate danger. The canisters were damaged but the vital supplies were usable. They cocked their Stens and lifted what they could and carried it near a hundred yards away. They pulled out the bodies and placed them under dark bushes. The plane they destroyed according to the instructions and flew into the woodland. A Lysander was still a mystery to the Germans and would have been very pleased to find one dropping into their lap.

The area they had roughly landed in was the Jura that was between Burgundy and Switzerland. The country was still very wild and ideal for the build up of resistance. T.E. Lawrence once described Resistance as an intangible and as a vapour, blowing where we wished; our kingdom lay in each mind. The rivers and mountains and the nearness of the neutral border of Switzerland seemed an ideal place for an offensive that would be near to invisible. Also there was the Peugeot car factory an ideal target in the Franche-Comte near to the Swiss border offering a juicy objective. In this region of two dialects an interpreter of some skill was required and this was met by Mat who had worked in the vine fields during the late 1930s. He joked that the North of the region spoke different dialect from the south and be still recognised as French. As they ran through the trees the moon as it was in pale lamination appeared and strayed while the ground did not reflect its aid to the night. Nearly out of breath Geordie slumped on the side of a tree that smelt of damp moss and let go the heavy sacks he had to carry. He panicked for a instant as he could not see them in the long tangled unlit grass. Mat saw a flash of light and the only conclusion was a German patrol so he quickly warned Geordie. Both shrunk to near the roots of the tree straining their eyes to see any movement that came towards them. A man wearing a cap raised his voice in a French call. By asking them to identify the two or be shot in a moment. Geordie knew that an answer was required in a short time responded by saying in English he did not want to be shot. That was enough for the recipient and a hand reached for his and shook it warmly. The safe place was full of guns and ammunitions and s single map placed in beside glasses of red and white wines. A carafe three quarters full caught the eye of Geordie and he signalled his interest. There leader was a large man dressed in a bulky leather coat cross banded with Sten gun rounds that gleamed from the candle light and clicked as he moved. He seemed pleased that this stranger liked a glass of the wine on his table. His eyes wore a sad look most of the time but now he had a spark of warmth. The first question he asked was whether they had children or not. Mat said he had one girl still a baby, the pride of his family who was the apple of his father's eye. Geordie not having any told the leader he had help save a boy and a girl in the London Blitz and sent them to Plymouth looked after by a responsible lady.

During a short leave he had visited the city that to his surprise had been also badly bombed. The lady had the sense to take the children out to the moor country and had lived in a small holding that she rented cheaply. It was a rough life that he admitted but so much better than the hell of waiting for a bomb to land on you. They were well and he was proud of their appreciation and he was glad to give them some food in cans and three large loafs of bread. When he left he felt a strong attraction for the first time in his life to stay with people he hardly knew and felt a strong responsibility. Geordie thought this must be the beginning to maturity he recognised the widening of his life force and the worlds true meaning. An attractive woman listened to Geordies story enthralled by his natural humility. She was their best man as the leader called her as she was fearless and dutiful. Her hair had a slight red and a blurry brown tinge that remarkably suited her brown eyes that danced when she spoke. Her lovers had been many and who never came back from raids leaving her empty until the next lover strolled into her life. Dvina was attracted to Geordie and showed it so plane the others were amused at her audacity. They thought they had seen everything but this it seems was different. Geordie was knocked out of sorts by this almost confrontational manner. He did not want to be seen as naive and at the same time too keen. His manners were pure British and he was as usual reserved. The weather was more interesting a subject in conversation that what was evident here. His heart was bursting and his senses retained a fraction of control enough to stay in tune with his countries morals. Dvina walked up to him and smiled before offering her bed. Taking his hand and took him like a child to the bed room. Geordie felt a thrill so profound it may have belonged to the cavemen. Once inside the bed room which was really a flour store, but what the hell whispered Geordie to himself as he lifted Dvina into his arms smothering her with love and the actions that followed all in a bundle of pleasure for both? There in the main room the others were in their own minds sinking to thought of feminine wonders and charms. Mostly they wanted peace and a secure life the rest they would take care of by themselves. The wooden house was warm and the local wines were scintillating and had the needed kick. Mat wished Austin were here to enjoying this time in the comfort of a good roof and a fire with good eats as Austin would have called them. Mat thought of Austin's family living in complete ignorance of his departure from the world. They would hold Christmas and place gifts for him to open on his return. Death seem so terminable so definite and blank. While life went on its merry way undaunted full of optimism just as Christmas celebrated peace and hope so death celebrated it victory by its terminations.

The next morning as rain came gently down and bounced from the leaves and trickled from the darkened barks to form a narrow minute tributary that flowed towards a deep lake. The men coming of guard felt the blood circulate that much better with the thought of food and strong coffee. Mat and Geordie had met to discuss their training plans so that the ones less clever would be able to follow. Jacob their leader and his second in command Igor counted the ammunition and the reliable weapons they had left. They called the group to see that they were fit and ready for a mission if needed. Szymon the youngest was the runner and was expected to race to with the speed of a gazelle owing to his long legs. He had wished to join the group despite his relations warning they would be shop in his place if the Germans discovered his identity and cause. They were a close proud bunch for all kinds of life unshakable in their beliefs of freedom and democracy. But this was so far away and so many things had to be done that the end of this war was a million years away.

The country was beautiful and the air had an aroma of wild nature as the autumnal sun began to warm the forests and fields. The trek was as long as it was described in the planning of the raid. The raid was on the car factory which although French had produced specific vehicles for the Germans. The spare parts due to war shortages were cannibalised from many old vehicles. The parts were skilfully knitted together to make various kinds of useful transport for all kinds of road and country. On the unhappy streets of Paris the last model they made was the in thing. It had an improved engine that made it the envy of other car makers throughout the rest of France. The model was seen by the enemy as ideal for the higher ups in the Nazi Party. This of course made it the perfect target for partisan devilment. They had trained over a three week period on weapons and tactics that to be honest the veterans of the group already knew, but were polite enough not to show their disinterest. Sitting attentive and taking in any new instruction on an instrument of death while the hours whittled away whilst the rain and wind battered the building. Geordie continued his lover fare under the eyes of the others quite innocent of criticism. Frankly he was blind to the world and so was his female counterpart.

On hearing Dvina had a twin sister it disturbed Geordie not just the fact there was two of them and if they were identical how would he be able to tell the difference. Mat advised he had got used to Dvina's body aroma and should find some excuse to try Colette. Geordie thought he would have to do exactly that to find a difference if any. He kept the idea to himself as it was sure to cause sparks and be the butt of the group's jokes for the next month at least. He had to admit he had some dreams that would be band to readers of the Times. During the tutorials and weapon demonstrations Geordie and Dvina slipped their hands to each other. He gave a warm smile to Dvina and she returned the warmth. One of the group an old farmer could stand it no longer and shouted, "For the love of God get married and give us all some peace, that would teach you." Everyone laughed with the exception of the two culprits. But the nights were human and full of delightful surprises disposing of bland wartime thoughts and lingering boredom.

Now they were in Indian line walking with arms at the ready, eyes looking sweeping across the surrounding area for signs of the enemy. Any noise including the sharp crack of a twig or a suppressed suddenly released cough made every heart jump and accelerates. Exhaustion crept in later as the evening came to an end as they climbed another interminable hill to fall down at the word, rest. The stars shone down innocent and sure of an eternity in blinks millions of light years away from the foolishness of earth's creatures. Geordie was sure the stars looked in melancholy at the two lovers and may have been rightly jealous of their closeness, while they were so far apart from each other. In the morning their feet were stone cold and moving was an effort just to take a few steps.

Soon they were warmed by a long hill climb and the light of a neutral sun and the news of nearing their target. In the fading light the last instructions were issued and the check of their equipment automatically signalled their imminent departure. Geordie and Dvina were allowed to be together as it was deemed to be cruel to separate them from each other. The smiled at each other as they moved into the coming night mist and trundled heavily along the narrow paths. They split up to smaller groups of five, silent and stealthy s as the inevitable barbed wire fence came into view. Geordie looked searching for signs of life and a possible observation and machine gun tower. He could see one about eight hundred yards away to the left which suggested there would be a foot patrol some time later. The wire cutters snipped a single strand which sprung dangerously near Dvina's face. Four struggled through the gap they had made, aware of their fatigue and vulnerability.

Geordie was last through and moved with more caution when he heard German voices coming nearer. He slipped into the longer grass and waited breathlessly. He wanted to cough his throat itched and his eyes filled. He had to shut his eyes and concentrate on the spoken words of the Germans. They were not in a hurry and stopped once or twice to find a smoke or exchange a photograph. Geordie thought in a few more seconds he would take his handkerchief and stuff it down his throat and die alone. He did not want to be a hero remembered for stuffing his hankie down his windpipe instead of attacking the enemy. But that would surely attract the other sentries not far away. During his inward debate the sentries started to run towards the machinegun post. He moved as quickly as possible through the wire gap and cast his eyes on Dvina. This was rapture entwined in relief and a heart full of happiness. He lifted himself up and ordered them to move along the disturbed grass route towards a copse of wild heavy leafy trees. He glanced at his watch and realised the time had flown and had to order them to make haste. The night had closed in quickly and the limit of vision had been reduced to about ten feet.

The rail line they were to destroy was built up on a shoulder of an embankment that was slippery. They crawled up on their hands and knees that slipped in unusual directions on the mud downward making progress slow and awkward. Geordie at first wanted to laugh at the clowning of those in front who slipped and found themselves facing backwards. In a short while they were on their feet exhausted by the slippery ordeal some spitting out clumps of grass.

At a moment's notice they carried out the tasks they were trained to do efficiently and silently. Not far from the machinegun post way there was the sound of a mob in a panic. Further down the track a car company rattled and puffed straining up the hill towards them. Geordie in the dark could hear the rail sing and knew it was time for them to take cover. Turning the magneto the explosion came a second after. It racked the night with sound and fire. The engine lifted off the tracks and fell on its side steaming in fury. A loud thunderous explosion followed the crash of wagons, spilling the heavy cargo into the dark long grass. The armed escort was nowhere to be seen but there was screams of distress that had to be ignored by the group. Geordie not used to the sounds of those dying in pain wanted to run and help. That he knew was impossible as the Germans were even closer that he thought. Their shapes began to appear in the light of the continuing flashes of explosions.

"One of us has to stay behind and protect the retreat." He was willing to stay if no one volunteered. He raised his voice to be heard over the racket and was brought to a halt when Dvina answered the call. "I will." "You can't do that." He heard himself shout as loud as he could. "Why not, I volunteered didn't I." Two of the men dragged him away down the mud slop and towards the wild copse. Geordie was stunned as the occurrence had happened in a trice. How on earth can she do that and what the hell I can do to run back and help her? I want to die with her; he rolled over in his mixed mind, while he was dragged strongly along. He wanted to scream and run crazy to her side, but he knew that could never be. Geordie heard the firing

162

and explosions of grenades and then a palpable silence that was an end to a huge part of his sole. He and the others had not said a word as they crept under the wire and along the long grass. The sabotage group crossed the river where it was almost ripple free, dark in places shimmering in others in the moonlight and now far from the cover of the trees. It was the ideal place for an ambush and Geordie felt naked and especially vulnerable as he groped with his feet for a good balance in the river that rose quickly up to his knees.

The sky was a varied roof of cloud and bundles of stars and a wide sanguine light blue on the distant horizon. Geordie knew it was the far off dawn and a new tomorrow that was sure to be as empty as a void. From the other side came flashes that stretched along the edge of the river. The splashes of the bullets whipped around his legs so much he wondered that at least one would hit him. He had to go back across to the other side and he called on the others to do exactly that. As he turned a bullet hit him hard on the side and twisted his body involuntarily around to drop into the sinister water. He drew in his breath and felt the cold water fill his lungs, then a rush of sights and sounds and ending in nothing. He was carried down the river till it bent around some large boulders. Geordie was washed in between two sharp rocks and caught upwards banging his head.

There was singing and what appeared to be a lamp light brushing his eyes and a feeling of water lapsing over his back. He opened his eyes and saw the sky of heavenly blue. There was the sound of birds happily whistling and chattering high in the trees. He was held like a vice in the rocks and blood that had dried on the back of his hand. He moved and an excruciating pain attacked his left side. He could hardly move but did so slowly and groaned at each progress. The bodies of the three men were lifting and falling in shallow ebb foamed water. They face down as if to hide their expressions. One had a hand that was reaching out and pointing at him. This was a sure sign he was to blame as he was the leader and the last breath of this man's life was to point at the accused.

It took two days for Geordie to make it back to the house camp. He at least had plenty of water and some chocolate in his pocket.

It was not much but he was sustained for the length of the journey. There was a joyous cry and many hands lifting his up. His head spun and the pain that had been unfelt became a rush of excruciation. He heard himself blubber out Dvina's name over and over before drifting to that end of consciousness. He could feel his heart beat powerfully and sure of itself. His vision came into focus and to his delight it was Dvina. Shush, shush rest its Colette her sister and I will look after you. "Collette, who the hell is that pretending to be my Dvina?" He continued to call this out for two long days and longer nights. Geordie began to settle into a warmer climate of less pain. He was more satisfied in his dreams and moments of awakening. He saw the face that he loved more often but called herself Colette. Soon he didn't care about a name as long as she is here and I could reach out and hold her hand. Slowly he became a human again and saw the world as it really was he began cautiously to talk to the girl who called herself Colette. Gradually he began to recognise subtle differences as in her sweet voice and the way she moved in feminine grace.

The love that he had for Dvina was transferred to Collette willingly as if it were meant to be. The magical miracle of life was back as powerful as it had ever been and Geordie was quick to propose to Colette before she was whipped away to the shooting war. Colette was happy to accept his wishes and both became inseparable. Mat reminded Geordie it was time to carry out part two of the mission by rescuing Robert.

41.

The limit of power is the endurance of its People.

A Lysander ran with its propeller speeding and lifted from the field. As planned from the beginning Geordie was on the way to Switzerland. Switzerland was an armed neutral country. It was the ideal place for planning sabotage in enemy Germany territory, in this case industrial espionage and if possible a rescue. As France had a similar border to Switzerland it was easily the best of crossing places. Switzerland had an open arrangement for the gathering of intelligence available to each side of the conflict and included practically every country that felt under possible threat or just were interested in counter intelligence. In the 1930s Switzerland had its own species of what was often considered Fascism but did not include Adolf Hitler and his contemplations of engulfing other countries. Most of the population did not trust the Germans and therefore resisted any ideal of being part of the Reich. Being so close to Germany they had access to the cruelty imposed on minorities, Jews and the disabled. The Germans had of course plans for invasion that was broadcasted as propaganda. It went "Die Schweiz, das kleine Stachelschwein, nehmen wir auf dem Rückweg ein" ["We'll take Switzerland, the small porcupine, on our way back home!"]. But there was one main drawback and that was gold and currency needed by the Germany. Also the Swiss apparently had plans to leave the borders if invaded and go to the Alps, a formidable mountain range that would have been difficult to occupy. But in truth this was a false threat that would have been difficult to do. But it was seen as a real threat to the Germans, and why destroys an excellent arrangement that was ideal for both parties.

Remembering, that 74% of Switzerland spoke German but unlike Austria they would have resisted even in defeat. With this in mind Geordie knew it would relatively safe in Switzerland. The intrusion into Germany would be a bit more of a danger. Landing in an isolated field covered by British Agents that were domicile in Switzerland was like a holiday to the Lysander crew. They were met with cheerful conversations and courteous backslapping.

The efforts of the British intelligence had paid off and swiftly Geordie was in a relatively safe house. It was not far from the place Robert lived which was a comfort to Geordie. Despite his good German language skills was still a bit unsure of his abilities and of how he would react to the first encounter with a Nazi official or just a curious Berlin citizen. The flight from Switzerland was during the night and seeing far below German isolated villages and roads carelessly lit. Were they ignoring the fact that they may be bombed any time soon or were they so sure of victory and life went on just the same? The drive through the bumpy side roads thankfully came to an end but the well built autobahn had continuous flows of military traffic each worthy of a nightmare of its own. He wondered why no one had stopped them and questioned them. The drive was not straight for Berlin it was in a circle crossing and passing points that were strongly guarded. The drive into Berlin was through still busy streets and shops displaying their wares. Cars and lorries were driven wildly and drivers busily tooting their horns gesturing threateningly just as they did in busy London, there was no real difference. The impatience and pressure of the traffic would have been difficult to investigate so Geordie suspected the authorities let it run naturally.

The rooms were spacious enough and were decorated in the pre first war German style showing the end of an opulence that was never regained. He lay in the bed looking out the large window as the lights of the traffic flickered across the wall and turned to a shadowy grey. He took out his note book he had always at hand as a journalist. He knew this was dangerous but old habits die hard.

The following days were more of recognisance and becoming inured to the customs of the Berliner. So far the information he would have send were of no military use more of a social study. The ordinary city dweller wondered how the Nazi war machine could not protect the capital city. Soldiers also wondered the same thing of why that confidence did not relay to the battlefield. Things were not so easy now. The German people had heard a person named Joseph Kennedy had sent to his American superiors, Germany had dominated Europe and it was futile for Britain to carry on. The Blitz was according to him the last straw that broke the camel's back. Despite Britain's propaganda there seemed no reason for the Germans to stop or to give up. All they had to do was keep up the battering until the British came to terms with the idea of defeat and that would be the end of the war. The American opinion was divided some believed in Kennedy's diagnoses, well he was the man on the spot.

Churchill's order to destroy the French fleet at Mers el Kebir showed a ruthlessness to continue the fight. The British had the bulldog spirit and would hold on and fight to the end. But the Berlin citizen did not quite see it that way there was an impact on their lives not only in the regularity of the bombing, it was the silence of the Nazi's in not explaining the reason for it. German soldiers were now stretched across the continent in so many theatres of war they were wondering where they would get the recourses to hold on to the captured ground. More important was the spectre of Adolf Hitler as leader of the world and their sacrifice of thousands of lives, was it really worth that. But and it was a giant but, the ordinary citizen could not for a minute see Germany as a defeated country, it had to win their leader had promised them didn't he.

German women formed groups to comfort each other in the long nights. When a bomber raid came and bombs fell randomly or carpeted and they crushed into shelters huddling together as one person. Their time in the shelters renewed the old optimism and congratulated themselves on an easy won war. When the all clear was sounded they trooped off home still warm in the bubble of comfort till they saw the tremendous destruction. They were working full out and were producing war materials as ordered and the whispers from some fronts were of lost causes and therefore some soldiers were not trying hard as they were. Still this would not be discussed in the open as it would have been fatal, it was not just a case of being branded as a traitor but more of a trip to a camp for execution.

A meeting with Robert was to be as soon as possible, it was now the passkey. This meeting had to look to those near enough to see the event as casual, like bumping into an old friend. It would be better in the dark and at a place where there were at least two escape routes. A corner street would be ideal and space to run close by. This was arranged and discussed to the finer points. Geordie set off looking forward to the meeting of his old friend his hand deep in his coat pockets, his right hand molly codling the pistol with the silencer it was the latest designed weapon for this kind of close contact warfare. It made him that bit more confident in the way a good engine was to a car. Robert was on the way to his flat held in concern for Egbert and the threat of the boy and his eavesdropping. He had recovered from his embarrassment and had doubled his interest in him and Vivienne. There was no doubt he was dangerous but his father and mother were such a nice couple the he was in a dilemma of having a conscience a lead weight to his heart. In the falling night and as they were in their own world they passed each other by and had not noticed. It was far down the road that Geordie realised the mistake. He huddled against a cold wall feeling the dampness seep through his garb. There was only one solution and that was to go to Roberts flat. This was a risk he was now willing to take as he felt he had been unprofessional. This foolishness had to be erased quickly. Geordies inward laughter at his whimsical attitude to an important war game showed at least he still had held on to his sense of humour. He shook himself shaking of the past and leaned forwards into the drifting droplets of fine rain. Berlin rain in the middle of a war and feeling a strange confidence and certainty he was going to do that thing he had been trained for and promised. Again he clutched his pistol feeling the cold and strength of the gun metal. He passed strangers not looking at them unless he had to, when he was in a place he was face to face with them he gave a look of a happy slightly inebriated Berliner on the way to a litre Steiner. At least that is what he had in mind. He held his breath for a second at the bottom of the stairway leading to Roberts flat and then pressed on. Forcing his legs to a faster rate he bounced up the stairs and held on to a rusty rail. The street from the front looked world class neat in appearance and tidy where as now hidden from onlookers an untidy array of flats with spilled rubbish so unlike the German dream. This was war and the importance was of hard industrial work not worrying about a little litter. He was at the door and immediately pressed without an instant delay. He heard the inside ring in a different planet. A more comfortable planet that the outside of wet and wind. He heard the footsteps of a woman dainty and feminine. The door was heavy and the lady had to pull twice to open it. Geordie was held by the sight of a wonderfully attractive woman with a confidant warm smile. He introduced himself to her and explained he had to see Robert as he had important news of him. Vivienne was curios and was ready to do something to the stranger to neutralise his being. She called Robert who strode into the lobby equally curious until he saw his friend. He was taken by surprise and with his jaw dropping and his eyes watering. He held out his hands saying, 'Geordie my old friend so good to see you here, but what in the hell are you doing in this den of iniquity. I have an excuse but you?' Vivienne relaxed and looked on in interest. 'Something very important to say in private.' Robert realising he meant Vivienne, he told him she was one of them. 'OK, you have to get out of here now this second as you are ordered to London.' 'But, but.' Robert was trying quickly to search for an explanation that was not coming. Then the penny dropped, he told Vivienne they must be on the way now. 'Don't take anything we leave pronto.' Egbert rushed into the lobby and nearly pocked Robert in the eye with his pointed finger. 'I have you now you rat.' Geordie lifted out of his coat pocket the pistol he had been coddling indulgently. He fired it at the head of Egbert and then his chest. Egbert dropped heavily on to the grubby carpet. Geordie snapped at the two and ordered them, 'now means now. They left closing the door behind wide eyed corpse of smug Egbert now worthless as he had been in life. Robert spared a second for the feelings of Erica and Gerard and the little sister Angeline. But only a second for now their lives were on the line.

The car drove through Berlin and mixed well with the days traffic tooting and exchanging insults as normal. Geordie told Vivienne and Robert about the new love of his life in such a serious manner both strained not to laugh. Naturally they felt a sorrow for the life of Dvina but Geordie was not the kind of man who had never been in the least romantic, so this was a new Geordie less constrained and more caring. Also he was far more decisive as they had just witnessed. The Lysander propeller swung into action and raced up the field to lift off the German ground with a powerful ease. The morning sky was radiant and heavenly tinted in blue to the horizon holding clouds of gold shimmering in the optimistic life giving sun.

42.

Russia in an unpleasant unplanned Retreat.

Cameron was invited to an evening's entertainment in the Garrison house of the Red Army. The Army song and dance group had arrived and Nichol Cameron's interpreter had run off to purchase a bottle or two of vodka in case the entertainment was not up to standard. Around the hall there was plenty of banter and laughter. Cameron had spent the last few days watching the new T34 tanks replacing the T26s; he thought it a little late in the day to make changes that should have been done months before. But they came in a constant drip with rushed training to fit them into the front line as soon as possible. The entertainers sang with great gusto an Old Russian favorite that sounded deeply melancholy and delightful to western ears. All through the performance Nichol glanced at him to ensure he was enjoying the fun. He handed the vodka to Cameron who took six long swigs and gulped them down, he stood up and swung his arms with the bottle of vodka held high proceed to join in the singing in totally made up words. Many officers and soldiers of the Red Army followed the enthusiasm of Cameron till the whole audience joined his appreciation of the entertainment.

After the performance according to an old army tradition they invited the artist for a drink and a meal. They danced and sang thought the night till near four in the morning. Both Cameron and Nichol threw themselves drunkenly into bed and immediately slept totally till they were awakened at six. They were both still under the influence of the goddess of vodka and had to stand under a cold shower for some time. Cameron was thinking about the German lines and wondered if they entertained each night as the Russians did helping to drive away the boredom of being so far from home. Nichol took Cameron on a tour of other red army formations and proudly introduced him after the previous night's entertainments to the Commanding Officers. There was a rumour the German top brass had a falling out about the plans to attack Russia. But General Ryabishev was sure Hitler intended to attack soon, while the Chief of Staff of the Army refused to believe it as the rumour had taken priority over common sense. They were convinced it would be another year before hostilities would break out. There seemed a strange dream like quality in the camps of not believing the inevitable and that the war was inconceivable. Even reality could be ignored while the vodka flowed and a game of cards was always in progress. The readiness of the forward units was more like something of a myth. Cameron already noticed the slow change of equipment and the procrastination of follow up training. He noted spare parts that were an imperative in tank battles were few in number. These faults had led to many a tragedy that had befallen so many armies of the past. Yet it was obvious to Cameron few took notice of histories warnings, which he felt were written in the stars. Nichol asked Cameron to accompany him to the see a popular General of this Army group, he happily agreed and ordered transport. They arrived just in time to follow the general to what they called the, workhouse, which was in fact their HQ. The name was joke to the staff; this is had once been the place they sent those who had failed in their duty for punishment. Amid the conversations a message arrived which did not seem particularly important; it was the usual, 'get ready and wait for further orders.' The order to 'stand too' was given half-heartedly while the clink of glasses proceeded with enthusiasm. Their Alarm Cases the officers of HQ were to carry on all occasions were casually placed on their desks, next to their weekend suitcases. Cameron had heard many complaining and grumbling voices that as Sunday was not so many hours away and that meant a day with the family or a trip to the local bars. Some even wondered if the concert was still on the Sunday bill and others had hoped there would be sports festival. But, whatever was happening was now a different time zone.

A general who had said he would cut his hands off if there was going to be a war was answering the phone, his head nodded up and down and his expression serious. His certainty of peace was still paramount. The message was stark of the German Artillery was being fired all along this front. The general was still convinced and warned his officers not to fire at any German aircraft until ordered. The day had begun in full swing when Cameron heard the sound of the tank engines staring up. He ran outside to see the morning sun aiding the German bombers, they were high overhead and clearly seen were the Balkenkreuz the German Empire cross on the aircraft upper wings as they dipped fearlessly unconcerned of the evidence of the attacker. They plunged down towards the railway station and began to bomb. Next were the roads and then the unprotected oil refinery. The barracks had been emptied some days before but were nonetheless complete destroyed. None of the Russian fighters were in the sky so the Germans seemed to bomb at their leisure. The prepared anti-aircraft gun sites were still silent awaiting the order to fire. And only when the Russians opened fire did the most pessimistic admit the war had begun in deadly style. Cameron and Nichol saw officers and the political men of the corps directorate standing in silence waiting for the general to say something, anything. But the general was in the same situation. He had no orders and there was stupefying silent. The laughing and banter had come to an end and there was no more moaning about the family Sunday dinner.

In the Balkan campaigns the Germans slow build up gave the impression that moving forces into place for another invasion would be the same. That the Russia campaign would take so much longer, or was the massing of forces a political demonstration of some kind? However, it was too late for the Russians to make up their minds.

At 03.00 on June 22nd the German lines from the Carpathian Mountains to the Baltic advanced while their aircraft flew inland and the thunder of artillery fire showered the ground with shaking destruction. The Russians put up a good fight at the Fortress of

Brest Litovsk and to the north. There were holdups crossing the river Bug even after assault bridges had been constructed quickly. It was the mud and marshy roads that caused delays. The Niemen bridges at Alitus were captured intact. Grodno fell on the 23rd June. The Russian airfields were attacked and suffered severe losses, this loss was a devastating set back to the defence of Mother Russia. Allowing the motorised units on the army's flank's to plan the encirclement of the Russians in the direction of Minsk. The Russian forces withdrew eastwards. The truck was full of smoke as the soldiers puffed their worries away. At times the truck would buck and tumble throwing rifles, kit and occupants over in assorted bundles. Cameron grasped the side of the truck swinging back and forwards, his hands were beginning to ache and arm muscles tighten. The mud tracks were falling behind into infinity over high and low hills and through swelling rivers. The sky had darkened quickly and clouds hung low almost touching the rim of what seemed perpetual hills. Cameron had been told the most popular book purchased by the German officers was 'Napoleon Bonaparte's Russian Campaign'. He thought, it's a bit late to read it now whilst on the way into a never ending Russia, coupled with the oncoming autumn that was only a few months off. It was not difficult for him to see the attraction of advancing at high speed against the Russians, ignoring the dangers of a fight back by a tired enemy. It looked as if the Russians had dropped the reins of an uncontrollable horse racing eastwards. German tanks were not far behind ready for an encirclement of steel against exhausted tattered flesh. During the night he could hear some groups resisting but there was no unifying leadership anywhere. There was no sign of surrender by the Russians, they fought on occasionally breaking the German encirclements were they were thinnest. This increased the German advance further into a never-ending country. Before he could tell Cameron of the deep rut they were about to fall into, Nichol felt the truck suspended in air before striking the solid mud. His first reaction was to save himself but gravity would not be ignored and he fell with force on to his face. The world vanished in a sickening thud. Cameron was still holding on to the side of the truck when he was wrenched from his safe perch. A rifle butt met him in the fall and a hand-grenade struck his temple. He could smell the iron of the truck and the damp wood seats along with human sweat as he slipped in and out of consciousness.

The Russians built strong defenses and used the thick growth as natural cover. Only the German infantry could penetrate the denseness of the forests leaving behind their armour protection. The blitzkrieg for the first time had to be modified to the extent of leaving the infantry to the mercy of the country. Ammunition and supply dumps had been left in places to strengthen the Russian resistance. Most of the Russian troops could live of the land and were not afraid of hand to hand combat. Even when engulfed in perfect panzer pincer the new Russian tanks counter-attacked the German lines so forcefully they allowed the escape of tens of thousands of Russian to flee north eastwards. Even in their greatest victories the unbeaten Panzer and infantry found it difficult to fully capture their enemy as it escaped and were very tough to follow. But with German persistence and gripping tactics they succeeded at Minsk. 300,000 prisoners were captured with 2,500 tanks cutting most of the Russian ability to escape from the pocket. But there was a penalty to pay the panzers had to leave behind about third of its force. This was to allow the infantry to catch up and relieve the panzers. With the loss of food and munitions they trooped onward in same direction. The importance German reserves were being used to sweep up the Russians left behind. This they only succeeded in partially. Cameron began to notice a general change in the Russian attitude. They seemed to be losing their stubbornness and began to surrender in larger numbers. He saw that Nichol began to appear lost and aimless. But with extra Russian persistence they moved off and Cameron followed. He took note that they were like winter birds flying to a certain place far in the distance with a stubborn certainty. Cameron had never known fatigue like this nor the gnawing hunger. He thought that the man in front had stacks of food hidden in his sacks and was even prepared to attack him in the night to eat his food, but sanity seemed to return in time. The roads were just as difficult for Cameron to negotiate as

Germans who followed. The dust was deep and exhausting catching the breath of the sweating soldiers clogging their pores of their body so that they felt like it was enclosing them. Their boots had become heavy with dust ballast making the soldiers trudge along at a pathetic pace. Water was becoming sludge and the result a mouth sifting the dust to satiate the continuing thirst. Cameron was not the kind of man to give in and he pushed himself along dropping into a phantasy or dream that came and went. He remembered the old man who lived near the shore for as long as anyone could remember. He had lived what seemed like three lives in complete happiness and the most elusive want of all contentment. Cameron was now with him sitting beside the old green door. Mat as he was called sat smoking his pipe before he worked the peat fields across the way. The land he had worked in was a clear patch that extended a fair distance donating the number of years he had toiled on it. A breakfast of oats and salted fresh fish or an egg and long streaks of ham accompanied by lumps of soft bread made by a neighbor six miles away. Mat hardly read a newspaper but when asked his opinion he would astound the asker with his sound sense of judgment. He would then apportion a few hours to his work in a steady pace, while stopping to look into the distance to fill his eyes with the sea and the rocky shores. The shore birds as they had always done screamed and dived into the cold deep. Some sheep had wondered along the side of the cliffs and Cameron wondered if Mat took advantage of this gift of free food. Mat would have answered truly but Cameron never asked as he might have let it slip to some enthusiastic law keeper. Any day he spent with Mat was almost identical with the exception of the weather which came and went like a kaleidoscope. If the weather took a turn for the worst as it did often with the howling wind and driving rain Cameron would be allowed to stay overnight or longer. Inside the cottage or ben it was warm and luxurious compared to a titanic battle outside. Mat had secured the windows and door so well they hardly moved in the constant battering and tearing of the end of the season's monster effort to scare every living thing. He was safe here and felt the sanctuary of this haven. But just as suddenly as he felt the safety he was knocked back to this reality so many times back and forward he was beginning to wonder what and where reality were. Cameron noticed Nichol had fallen and laid in stillness his body a lump of dust reminding Cameron of Gunga Din. He was still breathing puffs of smoky powder grime. With the remaining water Cameron gently washed Nichols eyes and wiped away the smears so that at least he looked human. Others tumbled by and some staggered into them cursing and groaning. Cameron pulled Nichol to a group of small trees that were over the rim of the road. A German tank rumbled by sounding victorious and dangerous. Screams could be head as the tank caught up with the Russian who lagged behind. Their bones cracked like branches and knocked under the metal of the tanks. The dark could not come quick enough as they huddled in fear listening to hurried German voices and tramping feet along with faster moving vehicles blasting monoxide over the road lip. Both slipped into sleep and were suddenly wakened to an eerie silence. Night had its charms in a cloak protecting them from the fieriness of others. Its stillness could be interpreted as an armistice of the heart. Nichol smiled at Cameron and wondered at the endurance of the Scots who were involved in every conflict since before Caesar of Rome in one way or another. He was sent as a journalist or a war correspondent and yet here he was miles from the others of his trade. They were probably living it up on vodka and plump chicken and listening to the latest salacious joke camped under a dry canvas smug in a bed of yielding feathers. And when sober they will write stories they were told by drunks and swear blind they were there.

While food and movement were the heart of the Russian effort, time was of the essence to the Germans conquest.

During a quiet period as the snow and rain mixed Cameron was asked in a brief and sharp manner to report to the nearest political Commissar Officer. Cameron didn't like the name and the type of person attracted to the office of useless pointless beings. They had the same rank as the military rank of the officer on the ground. Any decision had to be made between the two. The threat was always there of a political offence and the resultant firing squad. Cameron took his time not looking forward to the questionable order or inquisition. The commissar was as he expected well behind line and in a luxury of comfort well beyond the ranks and many officers. He faced a man who was dripping political idealism. A man who seemed so distant from reality he should have been sent home as a worldly joke. Cameron asked him to be brief and advised him of his own position of a news carrier not only to the Soviet Union but the world at large. The shells from the German artillery had a greater affect than any argument blasting huge holes along a few hundred yards target. The last few shells came so close that the ground underneath and above shook. The bottle of vodka and the telephone fell from a crumbling table knocking over a small insect like corporal who repeated the words spoken by Cameron. He was no doubt very intelligent and may have been brave but underground he was the exact opposite. He was advised to report to the Russian HQ as soon as possible which meant now. He was glad to get away from those creatures that were more dangerous that any shell. Cameron was not the kind of person to hold a grudge but he seen the result of political style destiny in war. When troops advanced with machine guns pointed at them with the order to shot those who were overcome by the enemy. There was neither allowance for tactics nor an allowance for a regroup. The allowance was for the gratuities killing of their own kind men and women. They were in practical terms the other enemy. Much would be made of the right during war but it was unnecessary as the Russian soldier's only needed training not shooting in the back.

The HQ was also in chaos like the rest of the front but there was a determination that he has seen in the field. The huge square general with an equally huge hat shook hands with Cameron heartily. He was sober and full of optimism and promise of a fearful welcome to the Germans. He gave Cameron a letter from the British echelon and the permission from the Russian intelligence.

43.
Istanbul a drink in the sun.

In a nutshell he was to make his way to Istanbul where he would meet a person or persons in a place to be advanced on arrival. Istanbul similar to Rome built on seven hills with a kind of midstream Mediterranean climate hot in summer and cool or cold in winter. Turkey was a neutral country in a world war that had dragged in many countries that had tried to avert war. It was similar to Lisbon full of refugees escaping the German invasion of their countries. The British had their own problems trying to balance the impossible mandate keeping a flood of Jews arriving in Palestine causing a war with the Arab population as if punishment for its great empire. Hitler had made a promise to the Grand Mufti in Palestine that no Jews would be allowed to escape to Palestine. The Turks were in a detestable dilemma trying not to allow refugee ships coming through the Black Sea. This was not a new problem as the Romanian Jews were persecuted long before the war by the Romanian Iron Guards. Thousands rushed to go to Palestine in coffin ships or fly by night shipping companies. A ship called the Salvador in 1940 registered as Uruguayan. It had no weather instruments, no compass and no life jackets with five times the ships capacity. In the Marmara Sea during a severe storm the ship sank. 327 passengers were in a space for 40. The ship sank on December 15th drowning 270 which included 66 children. 123 survived and 66 were sent to Bulgaria and none to Istanbul as they were picked up by the Darien 11 another refugee ship on the way to Palestine. Unfortunately the ship was captured by the British and the passengers interned preventing a Jewish Exodus. In time the Turks tried to arrange for the movement of Jews in US and

Britain without success, in every direction the war exacted term to prevent the any kind of happiness or freedom to an already distressed people.

Cameron had a cozy remit of recruiting Jews who would be of help the British to fight the German enemy and as a side line he would look after the monetary interest for the Russians where he could. This was in the shape of intelligence that Richard Sorge a fellow Journalist from Russia would save his country by indicating the Japanese would not attack mother Russia. Sorge noticed the Japanese were truly inscrutable but they had a flaw. This was at party time when they would talk freely dropping their guard. Sorge took full advantage of this weakness and found many Japanese secrets that helped his Russia. Sorge as a spy was probably one of the most effective in melting in with the military and populace arranging other covers for his work that seemed quite natural. But the final penance was never far away as a foreigner he was always under suspicion. And so would Cameron be a target to the suspicious.

There were many talented people who would affect the war and the future of the world. By a stroke of fortune Cameron met Dudley Clarke who was a master of deception with unusual methods and the probable instigator to the beginning of the commando concept of hit and ran or shoot and scoot. Previously, Dudley Clarke had had been arrested dressed as a woman not that this was particularly unusual. But stranger still was his release from prohibitions with the help of a German spy. There was one proper explanation of this method of ruse and that was to deceive an enemy but was there another to maybe entice some of the Germans into the game. The Hilton Hotel was quite luxurious and the place where anything could be provided for the right sum. Hilton was situated next to the German Consulate and as some spy mentioned to Cameron all doors were opened at convenient times provided you had the finance. The men and women of this spy business were usually smartly dressed and had a willingness to show their wealth and sophisticated manners. There were so many Hungarian upper-classes with astonishing titles the city with its colourfulness seemed like a Hollywood production. But so like Lisbon the problem is the falsity or the reality of information obtained by whatever means and sold or passed to the right authorities. A mistake or falsehood of material accepted by a country could be disastrous and the inevitable death to the operator involved. Also, the countries cost of lives of those involved in a world war fighting for their very existence. This is where Cameron knew the proper introductions were of extreme necessity. Not forgetting the ability to seem quite casual and fit in with this flood of information gatherers. The wooden halls and high leveled stairways of the hotel were classic shadowy places to meet people not simply by chance, where there was bound to be those wishing to make a change. The stairways led in the noisy and bright night club below. Below, were a myriad of circular placed chairs that sat beautiful ladies and men in smart suits and individually bright individual neck ties. It was as if was an exciting game worth the gamble. Some showed their education and wit gladly while others a bluffed their way through and often the most successful were those who used the simplest and almost foolish methods. Most nights were abuzz with those with a story to tell and a hint of adventurism. The price of Gold similar to Lisbon was diminished compared to real valid information. With the help of the many peoples of this once great empire intrigues were common in the backstreets and along the water ways. Istanbul contained Greeks, Sephardic Jews and other Jewish persuasions and nationalities with flocks of slave girls, including many dancing ladies from England. Cameron was amazed at the number British women skilled in eastern dances and their ability to fit in as if they were native.

Carla a Birmingham born Lady was one of those who had contacts with many of those with in power due to her beauty and wit. She spoke many languages and had that dark sensuous look expected of the indigenous people. Her real name was Carol MacPherson and her father a Scots Irish tradesman had expanded the whisky trade to this part of the world. "You have to find the contacts or your store of goods would diminish quickly and if you were foolish enough to find an enemy the Black Sea or Bosporus awaited you. In other word you had to be confident and be well-armed." He had a small mustache finely manicured and a hair style that could accommodate his lack of hair at the back of his crown. He wore Middle Eastern flowing cloths and carried a jeweled yatagan Ottoman Turkish knife. Cameron wished he had the same ability to appear eastern but Carol was six foot six and gave an appearance of a far from easy adversary. Carol had one characteristic that interested Cameron and that he was left handed which indicated both sides of his brain were similarly developed and balanced. In his limited experience he had deduced Carol would be quick and decisive but hoped he would never find out.

Cameron not a keen smoker puffed a little on his coloured cigarettes barely touching their gold tips. But he was drinking more than normal and suspected those at his table were noting that fact. The best of brandy and whisky festooned the table. He noticed his drinking class was continually being filled as if by magic. He had this presentiment that they were determined to find him a bit tipsy and verbally excessive later in the evening. Mr. Dudley Clark, always at your service Mr. Cameron said a voice almost shouting in Cameron's ear as his senses began to drift like the smoke abound around him. Clarke's reputation to those in intelligence was well known but less so how much his strong influence in military matters. He had learned to fly in Egypt and at the end of the war in 1919 he had varied intelligence occupations in the Middle East and in 1936 help organise an answer to the Arab Uprising. It could be said he was not only the father of the Commando principle but also the SAS and the American Rangers. He was often considered to be the Greatest British deceiver of the Second World War and involved in so many strategies and ideas he was nothing if not a sagacious.

Through Lieutenant Colonel Dudley Clarke of MI9 or "A" force, Cameron was introduced to Adem and Beyza of the Turkish Intelligence who were involved the interest of the sale of Chromite an ingredient required for the manufacturing of stainless steel and selling it to Germany. The Turks also supplied it to Britain that naturally competed with Germany over the Chromite orders although in truth they could manage from other sources. It was a case of out matching the industrial might of the enemy. Just how much monetary intrigue was in those deals was probably enough to satisfy many a character. M19 was building a web in that part of the world not only to find intelligence that would be to the advantage of Britain but to help in the escape of prisoners of war which the including allied pilots. Cameron, with Clarke's persuasion found some in MI9 who would help in other fields of intelligence and gained a broadening of his remit. Clarke on the other hand on a return to Lisbon posed as a journalist for the London Times called Wrangal Craker posing as a journalist for the London Times to spread rumours to Berlin this may have been a strengthening of his "A" force deception plans. Dudley's lover fare lasted to the end of the war.

To Cameron, Clarke seemed to have an image of himself as a comic adventurer that probably began in Ladysmith during the Boar War when he was still a child. Clarke later tried to claim a campaign medal while still an infant at the time. But whatever the reason he was one of the best we had and his discrepancies were at this moment irrelevant. His secret "A" deception force was now being established in London but Clarke out of his loyalty to the Middle East refused the more important London governmental position. Later Clarke was on the ship Ariosto when the convoy was torpedoed by a U-Boat. His ship was one of three ships sunk. After this incident he was brought under the control of London who realised his importance wanted him to curb his dangerous wondering habits.

Most evenings Carla and Cameron had many talks on of what could be an effective way in helping the allied war effort. It would be doubtful if they would get authority in such a plan. What was on their mind was the possibility of mainly the release of Jewish scientists or chemists trapped in Istanbul. They knew there was a danger in looking for Jews in the streets and asking the wrong kind of questions to the wrong people. It was near the impossible to be right in a country that was in such a transition. So like the chameleon changing colour according to the environment or threat it was under at the time.

The Jewish haters in Turkey could not be contented no matter what. To many of them the Jewish people did not willingly carry weapons to protect themselves and were therefore considered cowards. Even among themselves Jews were not sure they should protect themselves as they had been suppressed by so many years of anti-Semitism and blatant discrimination by the Turkish authorities. There was the continual pressure to become a Turk and to assimilate not only as a condition but as a human being. When they did successfully assimilated they were more economically viable than their Muslim neighbours, to Cameron it was the final insult to a hardworking populace.

In May 1941 labour battalions conscripted non-Muslim persons a concept that went back to the Balkan Wars (1912-1913). Jews were now looked on by the Turks as potential fifth columnists and supplied with picks and shovels instead of weapons. The German Army having conquered most of the Balkans and was now in place to threaten Turkey. The consequences were an unhealthy relationship with any they may consider potential enemies. The threat was very real to the Turkish People increasing as the war progressed.

Business existed in this atmosphere of threat and violence; it was a driving force of nature that transcended fear. The odorous streets where many of Jews competed every minute of the day to exist were so far removed from normal living. An alarm passed though the crowds would be sent should an inquisitive approach be made from the lights of the Spanish Embassy to the river side. Cameron stuffed a bundle of many in is coat pocket and reloaded his pistol after feeling its weight, as if to reassure himself a bullet was heavy enough to kill. Carla not gun shy checked her fancy silver gun carefully and immediately turned to the mirror and glanced at the face that looked back at her. Her looks were insurance to her as an extra pistol or a hidden dagger. Cameron on the other hand ruffled his hair in the approximate direction. He then put his hand inside of his coat and slid it to a waist Lugar Pistol as a second string weapon. He loosened its strain on the leather holster and checked the safety catch. It was best to do this carefully as a mistaken shot in the lower half of the trunk may be deadly.

The streets were comfortable with a very slight drizzle as the evening light faded. The Fennel part of the city had its multitudes of lamps and tall buildings and twisting tall streets where Cameron felt claustrophobic in the narrowest alleyways. In the back ground he saw the city walls built by a Byzantine Emperor Thedosius so long ago. He admired the outward remains of the magical style of the Pera Palace which had been acquired by some illicit means by a Greek, which was not altogether a surprise to Cameron. The hotels history was full of the same intrigue as war time where Mustafa Kemal to be known later as the Ataturk had tried to convince the British they had something's on common. But only a few weeks ago the Pera Palace was bombed damaging the interior. This was assumed to be done by an Axis Bulgarian hoping to finish off a British diplomat. While others blamed the Jews who had been heard talking in the Bazaar and bragging of the spoiled palace and its now useless remains. It was said the bombing was done in the pretext of a Bulgarian revenge attach where as it was a Jewish scheme to see how far they could go in acts of great vandalism as a revenge for Turkish cruelty. But, as Cameron knew in this city of intrigue any whisper became a thunder rolling over commonsense. He could in his imagination see the Russian Princesses flirt with the British Officers after the Russian revolution and the affairs that led to success and fatalities. In an opulence that he a Scot could only dream of incomparable and dreamlike.

44.

Sweet and Primed.

In the Egyptian Bazaar was so like a stone Maze with its high structure amid the aroma of the many spices on daily sale in the complexity of shops. The exception was the Grand Bazaar where business raged on in an unending competition all within the thousand shops displaying every colour known to man. Under the lights the colours remained distinctly bright and gave out their own luminosity. In one square a band of Jews huddled together chatting ten to the dozen while keeping a look out at the same time. Carla and Adem one side and Beyza on the other, approached six of the group situated in the centre of the square. They listened intently while eyeing up the two tall men suspicious of their apparent power. They asked her to come back later and they would give a definite answer to her questions of false trading of Chromite and the possibility of find and the escape of scientist to Britain or America. The four sipped a very strong coffee from a small golden cup. Carla had mint leaves in her coffee and Cameron a drop of brandy he had persuaded the Inn keeper to depart with for a small fortune. There was an interest from all round not because of their non-oriental looks but the time of day. The sun had vanished and all the lights of the Bazaar illuminated the shopping area as if it were daylight. The night bazaar it seemed belonged to the locals and the lit embassies, clubs and hotels belonged to the infidel.

With the overcrowding the Jewish people were looked on as piranhas that came into the world armed with sharp teeth. Cameron did not understand the concept of a dangerous fish to a good Jewish lawyer or doctor. Last week the Synagogue Etz Ahayim was set alight and the Bazaar buzzed with schemes of deliberate murder of a holy place. He held Carla's hand as they strolled back to the square and talked to each other as if they had been friends for years. He noticed that she was bolder than him in many aspects and it showed in the way she openly revealed her opinions. In fact she did not care one way or the other what others thought. A characteristic Cameron wished he had, it was evident to his very being Women were the dangerous and most inventive of God's creatures. As they came to the square she carefully checked her pistol in fashion he would have expected form a Marine but then he really did not know her. She was sweet and primed and he could feel it. They sat quite informally within the group of Jews and waited some kind of communication that was continually being delayed. This came as a rush of Turkish Hajduk one clan known for their lack of mercy and their ability to frighten the law. The largest must have been seven foot and he used his expanse to sweep away the sitting peaceful Jews. With cuts across their faces and arm they ran crouched to avoid the vicious blade. Two fell and were finished off swiftly. The others ten Hajduk were swinging and thrusting while two fired semi-automatic guns into the sitters. Adem was hit badly and Cameron dragged him out of the square and placed his back against a pillar. Carla felt her back being burned by a passing bullet and turned to drop on of the Bandits with one shot in the teeth and another in his heart. Cameron was now behind the Hajduk on a blind flank. He fired into the thickest of the group. Arms flew in the air and unexpected screams filled the lantern lit Bazaar. The giant came for Cameron as quick as a viper and lifted his sword as he moved as in for a speedy kill. Out of the subfusc shade between the high pillars Mr. MacPherson appeared as the angel of death. He produced a Webley mark IV Pistol that blew the hand off the large Turkish bandit. The sword swung through the air and clattered clearly in front of the remainder of the gang. It was to the Turks an apparition from hell as the Webley blasted again and again killing the two Sub Machine Gunners one who was so shocked he threw the Sub Machine Gun in the air and tried to catch it but had left his mortal coil in that instant. Mr. MacPherson stood defiant with his white Arabic cloak floating in the air like a pair of wings. His short sword struck out to a wounded man and sliced of his ear. Cameron aimed his pistol and fired at one of the running men. The bullet hit his calf and he screamed and repeated his jump before landing in a heap begging for mercy. Cameron had expected the police to come running in arresting them all but that was not to be as they were apparently busy elsewhere arresting a donkey and cart smuggler of unlawful beverage. Adem was hurriedly taken to the Hospital and attended to by the best doctors they could buy. He was more than pleased to be alive and that was exactly the sentiments of Cameron. Cameron noticed those who were treated for less serious wounds made more clamour, including himself.

On returning to the Hilton they were met by the circle of well-known spies who plied them with drink and questioned their every moment. They were the Hilton Hero's for a day and took full advantage of the situation calling for the best of food and drinks for everybody. Later six Jewish university professors arrived only to find the tables strewn with bottles and food. The people they were given orders to meet stealthily were unconscious like rag dolls arms outstretched over the tables or horizontal on the floor. The professors looked at each other and nodded in agreement. Then threw themselves on the plentiful uneaten food. In the dim light of early morning they staggered to their rooms with their company of professors and threw themselves on to a bed and snored like thunder so much they were cautioned by the hotel manager at dinner.

Carla and Cameron discussed the question of Zionism and what it meant to the Turks. A Zionist education and tradition was connected to Israel which prevented the youth from assimilation. Even when the parents of Jewish children no to wear the Star of David in a public place and to say silent this was often impossible. To make matters more byzantine the pre War Turkish Government issued a decree 11 times prohibiting entry visas to Jews escaping the Nazi regime. But so many of the Jewish people in the Middle East saw Israel as the only light of freedom and democracy in the mist of darkness, terrorism and hatred in the region. The thought of an eventual country inspired the Jewish people to take whatever chance need, to reach their haven.

Cameron had enough of spying and intrigues more to the point he was sick of listening to those who fought a war on their backside. While they passed time sipping expensive drinks and talking the days away instead of a life of action, it was comparable to Cameron to reading a book about mountain climbing and actually doing it. He applied for a release from the spy prison and a return to Russia. This was accepted and he was to return to the same front he left. He said his goodbyes to Carla and wished then luck in the future. Her exotic loveliness and her British accent captivated his desires. In all honesty he had fallen in love with Istanbul and secretly made contacts for later years to purchase good properties before the war was over. This was not difficult after the contacts he had made during his short visit. But the troubles of finding transport to Jewish homeland continued.

In 1942 The Struma was taken out to the Bosporus laden with Jewish refugees. The Turkish engineers on board abandoned the ship in the Black Sea with the engine not repaired. As it sailed along some passengers hung a sign 'SAVE US'. About ten miles north of the Bosporus the ship drifted and came under the eye of Shch-213 of the Red Fleet and was sunk. Many of the passengers were trapped below and were drowned. Others by finding pieces of wreckage survived. 799 were lost including 100 children. Needless to say the British were blamed but one of the sailors the only crew survivor held in Turkish custody was given papers by the British to go to Palestine.

45.
The long march in Russian Soil.

What was certain in Cameron's life was the threat of the German drive to Kharkov. The Germans swept towards Kharkov the forth city of the Soviet Union. Hitler had mistaken the ability and staying power of the Russian peoples when he made a speech about kicking the door down. Smolensk south of the town would be a German victory at great sacrifice. The Russian tactics were of fighting in what seemed layers, preventing easy movement to the enemy. The complete battle raged for two months from July 10th to September 10th 1941. Now 18 days of invasion had passed without too much resistance till then. The German encirclement south of Smolensk destroyed the Russian resistance but as previously noted significant numbers of two armies managed an escape. On the way to Moscow a prime target was the town of Smolensk where the Soviet troops under Field Marshall Timoshenko now held with a smaller army. It was after all September and Cameron noticed the weather elements had become as part of the daily resistance to movements as the autumn rains had begun. The Russian Commander called the officers and as many men as could be spared and explained that the next great move from the German was the industrial conquest of eastern Ukraine. He told the exhausted army the aim of the enemy was the 60% of Russian coal 30% of its iron and 20% of its steel. The majority of its chemical factories and three fifths of the soviet rail system that carried a main supply of oil ran in the eastern end of the Ukraine. The capture of this part of the Ukraine would cripple the soviet any efforts to rebuild the war losses they had so far entailed.

The soldiers next to Cameron were definitely weary and leaning against anything near that could hold their weight including each other. A German victory in the caucuses may bring Turkey on to the German side and a Soviet victory may bring Turkey on to the side of Russia so the situation was vital and dangerous. Also the factories the Russians were so good at moving and rebuilding further east was now in danger due to the loss of manpower and the loss of equipment. The General looking equally tired pointed on his map the position of the enemy armies. Six German and Rumanian armies with Hungarian, Italian and Slovak troops equaled another army. Timoshenko was in deep trouble as in one of his tank units had only one tank and his artillery could only make a reserve from other army units sending them their artillery pieces. Both Armies now saw the summer slowly vanish and wheeled vehicles became useless and were now using horses and oxen to draw heavy equipment. The Soviet air force targeted those beasts of burden to slow down the pace of the war the Germans had as an object to their tactics. From 12 to 15 miles a day in good weather to 1 or 2miles hung over the German Command likened to a darkening shadow. Von Rundstedt thought they should avoid the larger towns despite this pushed into Kharkov as the main Russian force pulled out in good order with better tactics. In the beginning the Soviets relied on line tactics but they were vulnerable to break through by the panzers. The Soviet 9th Army was charged with the defense of Rostov and this time used better methods. The Defense consisted of four lines one behind the other. Next the anti-tank guns with interlocking fields of fire. Machine guns dug in intermingled with dummy dugouts. Guns were flexibly situated to turn if needed. Then other defensive positions were built so that a new position could be used quickly. The infantry had narrow trenches so they would not collapse and the tanks would go over the trenches while the Russians attacked the coming Germans. Banks of streams and creeks were undercut at natural crossing places. Along with tank traps on the flanks the main roads were mined. Then came the open ground and another defense to eventually the 9th Army defensive was around 50 miles deep.

Von Rundstedt rested before the major attack on Rostov. The 9th army that was to outflank the city was not going to plan and Rundstedt knew of Russian reinforcements nearby. Because of this the Germans changed their plans some troops were left behind in case of a counter attack. The 1st panzers sophisticated style of encirclement had failed miserably so an old fashioned frontal attack was carried out successfully. But news from the troops left behind was not good as they were under attack methodically. The Russian reserves were called in and the first time in the Second World War the German Army was called on to face an enemy attack. At this point the great scales of war began to tip fractionally against the German Army. Their high command began to think seriously of the Russians as their men they poured into Rostov were heading for a noose that was tightening. Still the 1st Panzers pushed gradually into Rostov. Cameron and his Russian comrades were facing the elite SS Viking Division. This elite division was slowly pushed back in the north east. The city was ablaze and the stench of the burning bodies, tank fuel and high explosives rented in the November air. The artillery had preceded the tank attack and blasted much of the city making it turmoil for some of the tanks that were launched from the Russian tank traps. Cameron saw the underbelly of the tanks in the distance rise from the ground and proceeded to fire their guns as soon as they were able. The Germans had to dig or untangle each obstacle as they advanced while under the Russian artillery shells. While the Russian tanks came on to the scene some were destroyed by the Panzers almost immediately. Now the German soldiers rushed the forward positions and Cameron all too soon found two German assault troops jump into the slim trenches, to his right a grenade exploded killing the German who probably threw grenade while the other one dived on Cameron. He was struck with such force he was knocked on his back. A hand to hand fight with all its dangerous twist and turns and tumbles and screams that came to Cameron came like a scene from a war movie. He was so shocked he found it difficult to find this reality. A knee in the face that brought blood from a crunched nose brought on Cameron a kind of wild fury that made his limbs stronger. The

German was young and fit and knew exactly what he was doing. Cameron found a slate stone in the newly dug trench and spun it around in the air and drove it into the Germans throat. Not satisfied by the blow that brought blood and air drooling from the Germans mouth he struck the eye and mouth. A shot rang out from above and the German was dead shot in the chest. There was no time to thank the shooter as he crawled out nearly being crushed by a Tank. The Stuka and fighter planes bombed the front trenches while machine gunning the Russian troops as they ran. Many stayed behind in the narrow trenches to catch the infantry unexpectedly. Cameron through his German field glasses he acquired recently. He saw the main advance party wait while the Stuka bombers screamed down on the unfortunate defenders. The industrial buildings and where troops massed were the first points to attack. It struck Cameron as he looked over towards the enemy they were so casual as if they were lining up to play a part in a movie. Those in armoured cars appeared to be talking, smoking and laughing as well as pointing in to the distance towards them. As the troops making ready for the advance piled over into the trenches and lay in rows with some cigarette smoke rising into the grey sky. This must have been done many times in battles of the recent past and now just a part of an eventual victory. Cameron thought but this time it must be different. The imperative was to slow them down or the major cities of Russia were within distance of a serious assault in the next few weeks. Cameron saw the masses of panzers moved forward quickly shooting exhaust fumes. The troops sat on top some evidently smiling as they had a free ride to the front and the support of the Panzers. The troops began to set fire to buildings as the lumbering panzers fired point blank into the office blocks while troops jumped to the ground and lay on the road side protected by a rise in the ground.

The machine gunners fired into the German soldiers who much to their surprise had some local Russian boys working along beside, this was probably in the hope of gaining food. Some had German uniform parts making indistinguishable for the rest. Cameron did not have bad feeling towards the boys who must have been starving and frightened. Artillery battles began to build up as the regiments of infantry came in range of each other. The SS Viking Division could not hold its ground this was unimaginable to the German high command. But in another effort the Germans began to advance towards Cameron who was fighting on the edge of Rostov. His accompanying units fighting for each patch of ground and building block felt the force of this new attack. His companions were ready to die for Rostov but he was wondering if this was worth it. He was covered in mud and his sight was blurred with pieces of flying dust. His submachine gun was hot from killing a group of Germans spilling from a tank. It reminded him of France. There the Germans were piling from trucks without thought of enemy preventative actions. It was a drill and had to be followed and made them easy targets for that moment. But soon he was overwhelmed and grenades flew through the air some exploding in flight. His ears began to hurt and his eyes burned with dust that caused a loss of direction. He was not sure which way to go and was ready to shoot at whatever looked dangerous. The German soldiers increased in volume most hugging the buildings where they could as the rest advanced fearlessly. At this point Cameron ran into a group of Germans huddled near a front door. He used all is guile to smile at them and made through the door which swung on its hinges and fell with almighty clatter. The dust piled up as a shell landed inside throwing the insides including Cameron against the walls. An artillery gun swung around to fire inside the wide open space of the door. A shell landed near its right wheel and its five man crew disintegrated in a red mess. The shrapnel from the metal of the gun hit the soldiers near the door causing some to fall in a heap and others cover their eyes and stagger around. Lines of German soldiers walked towards the centre of Rostov passing burning tanks. Small hut size houses with wooden fences shook as blasts of heavy artillery softened the ground for their advance.

Cameron just barely conscious and took the wrong end of the building which led to the town centre. He held his head with one hand and rested it against the wall. He saw the larger building you would expect to find in city squares burn. Snipers fired from high up and caught soldiers who ran around for a moment and then began to fire back. Other soldiers carried on as if nothing was happening. He tried to run and fell over a body lying over a tram line. Staggering and shouting Molina's name he turned a corner to see the Rostov centre being stormed by the German infantry. They rushed forward bent almost double innumerable like ants. Soon the Russian defenders walk out of building and lift their hands up in surrender. Cameron found motor bike that had slipped on the tram lines. He lifted it up and kicked it. Then kick started it with a warm roar. He was off knowing the opposite direction which he hoped must be the right one. The Germans seemed to know the sound of their own machines and ignored him or waved. Cameron waved back, he could hear them laughing as victory fell to the III Panzers. It was their city.

But to the north the Germans fell back and for the first time the Germans came near to become encircled by the Russian shock troops that had just joined in the attack. They were pressing down on the German flank and rear. The result was the Germans could not now a make break out of the south of Rostov. They had destroyed the bridges and the Russians of the 65th Impendent army held fast. General Cherevichenko knew of the possibilities of encircling the Germans but it was a big but, the Red army was short of mobile units and its infantry scares of men. There was only one solution to the General and that was to recapture Rostov. The result would be a blow to the Germans and on the international front the Turks would find joining with the Germans less attractive. The Russians attacked took time to organize. It was decided to attack in three groups. A company of the 33rd Motorized Rifles crossed the Don on the ice forming a small bridgehead in Theater Square. They found Cameron leaning against a tall bear tree. He was Just 200 yards from the Theater Square. Cameron was more dazed than injured and volunteered to go with the mortised unit. Two battalions of Militia after crossing the Don captured the Cement Factory. The ice was not thick enough to carry heavy weapons or tanks but enough to allow more troops to cross. The attack was all the way along the Tuzlov River. The 1st

Panzers held off the attack in their area and held open a corridor to allow an escape but had to commit all its reserves.

Rostov was abandoned before the Russian reserve arrived. It had been held for only eight days. A large Russian force chased the German army and Von Rundstedt knowing that Hitler would not permit a retreat resigned on the spot. Germany's most famed soldier left the Eastern Front.

Despite the glorious victories of the summer months the brilliant maneuvers and the nearness of Leningrad and Moscow the Germans faced massed Soviet divisions and to add to their difficulties a bitter winter was already on its way.

After the third phase of the Battle of Rostov offensive operation ending on the 2nd of December 1941 when Hitler countermanded Von Rundstedt order to retreat, just five days later the Japanese bombed Pearl Harbour. The antagonism between Japan and America was not new it belonged to another time. During the 1915 when Japan issued its Twenty one demands on China that would ultimately give Japan a special status and privilege in specified part of the country. This demanding move was in direct conflict with the Open Door policy conferred by the United States regarding China. All countries had to respect Chinese sovereignty and enjoy equal access to the countries trade. The economic problems of the late 1920s and the great depression had spread throughout the world and in particular affected was the island country of Japan. Japan was over populated and short of natural recourses. America had closed the door to Japanese emigrants along with its trade difficulties it therefore saw China as an ideal solution. Manchuria was undeveloped and the Chinese import market could be dominated. The Japanese build a railway in Manchuria increasing their ability to transport goods and troops at higher speeds. The invasion of Manchuria began in 1931 and led to full out war in 1937. Despite American diplomatic efforts the Japanese went ahead. America forced limited economic sanctions on Japan and gave military assistance to China. Naturally Japan resented the sanctions and military help given to China. In 1939 the Japanese were bogged down in China and could not change their stubborn refusal to submit. The German quick victories of 1940 enticed Tokyo to emulate the German successes and attack a number of seemingly defenseless territories in South Asia and the South Pacific. The American government increased its sanction on Japan which included oil imports which lead to the possibility of leaving Manchuria. This was a direct insult to the Japanese military and lead directly to the attack on Pearl Harbour with the hope of a quick victory. The news of the attack was broadcast throughout the world with a mix of disbelief and relief.

Cameron woke up after two days and nights of sleep. A large Russian came to his bed side. He put his large hand on his shoulder. "My son you have been shouting a girl's name and the boys want some peace, it's time for you to go to Molina before someone shoots you." Cameron agreed and left that night feeling the Russian army was right it was time to see his girl.

There was still a long way to go but Rostov gave the Russian army time a most valuable element in war.

46.

If you go anywhere, even Paradise, you will miss your Home.

The mist was thinning on the purple and green hills and the song of the skylarks rotund and joyful. The small neat cottages everywhere had new painted rickety fences and in their perimeters busy clucking chickens selecting fat worms and wildly fallen grain from the brown dry warming ground. The farm workers were tanned and healthy as they walked side by side with the plough horses that lifted their white hooves and clumped them down certainly, lifting a smudge of dust. The trees were heavy leafed and the crows high up were celebrating the pleasing morn.

Cameron lifted his tired eyes and studied his friends. Molina was lovely beyond measure and held his heart amenably; Geordie was swaying sleepily with his new girl Colette. He was now strong and mature and held her into his body. Robert and Vivienne were like an old married couple as a single unit that could never be properly defined. Larry, as swift as a cheetah and as strong as an ox his dog collar loose dangling casually and the bible had had been devouring lay on his knee patiently. David, Cameron's father was greyer on top as if someone had thrown ash over his head. His advancing years combined his slim physical body with the distinct features of a country doctor. He was complimented in his life by his wife Clarinda truly the mistress of his soul spot on to the word of the Bard. In all they were once again together and content. In Molina's cottage homely and sheltered they indulged in a local smooth whisky and a complimented the ladies with a toast. Robert and Geordie were obliged to call in for another war operation. Cameron lifted the phone to call the British intelligence section named the MARTIANS.

198

Printed in the United States
By Bookmasters